Melissa Lawrence swims ashore in Australia. She has no idea what to expect after escaping her captors. Since becoming Mel Lawrence, she finds her interests are expanding beyond just the "woman of means" role she had been raised to accept. After finding someone to teach her about becoming a grazer, she herds a flock of sheep into the Australian outback. She never imagined she would find a mate, a land that challenges her, and a life she felt she was bred for.

A K'Anne Meinel novella

Novels in Paperback:

SHIPS *CompanionSHIP, FriendSHIP,*
RelationSHIP
Long Distance Romance
Children of Another Mother
Erotica
The Claim
Bikini's Are Dangerous
The Complete Series
Germanic
Malice Masterpieces 1
The First Five Books
Represented
Timed Romance
Malice Masterpieces 2
Books Six through Ten
The Journey Home
Out at the Inn
Shorts
Anthology Volume 1
Lawyered
Malice Masterpieces 3
Books Eleven through Fifteen
Blown Away

Blown Away
The Alternate Cover
Small Town Angel
Pirated Love
Doctored
Veil of Silence
Malice Masterpieces 4
Books Sixteen through Twenty
The Outsider
Pirated Heart
Recombinant Love
Survivors
Inn the Dog House
Flight
An Island Between Us

Vetted Series:
Vetted
Cavalcade (Prequel)
Pioneering (Prequel)
Vetted Further
Vetted Again

Novellas in Paperback:

Mysterious Malice (Book 1)
Meticulous Malice (Book 2)
Mistaken Malice (Book 3)
Malicious Malice (Book 4)
Masterful Malice (Book 5)
Matrimonial Malice (Book 6)
Mourning Malice (Book 7)
Murderous Malice (Book 8)
Mental Malice (Book 9)
Menacing Malice (Book 10)
Minor Malice (Book 11)
Morally Malice (Book 12)
Morose Malice (Book 13)
Melancholy Malice (Book 14)
Mad Malice (Book 15)
Macabre Malice (Book 16)

Marinating Malice (Book 17)
Macerating Malice (Book 18)
Minacious Malice (Book 19)
Meddlesome Malice (Book 20)
Meandering Malice (Book 21)
Vaquera Safica (Spanish)
Surfista Safica (Spanish)
ケーアンヌ・マイネル (Japanese)
Maniacal Malice (Book 22)
Sayyida
The Northwood Lodge
Monitoring Malice (Book 23)
Marked Malice (Book 24)
Shanghaied
Outback Born

Pocket Paperbacks:

Mysterious Malice (Book 1)
Sapphic Surfer
Sapphic Cowgirl
Meticulous Malice (Book 2)
Mistaken Malice (Book 3)
Malicious Malice (Book 4)
Masterful Malice (Book 5)
Matrimonial Malice (Book 6)
Mourning Malice (Book 7)
Murderous Malice (Book 8)

Mental Malice (Book 9)
Menacing Malice (Book 10)
Minor Malice (Book 11)
Morally Malice (Book 12)
Morose Malice (Book 13)
Melancholy Malice (Book 14)
Mad Malice (Book 15)
Macabre Malice (Book 16)
Marinating Malice (Book 17)

In E-Book Format:
Short Stories

Fantasy
Wet & Wet Again
Family Night
Quickie ~ Against the Car
Quickie ~ Against the Wall
Quickie ~ Over the Couch
Mile High Club
Quickie ~ Under the Pier
Heel or Heal
Kiss
Family Night 2
Beach Dreams
Internet Dreamers
Snoggered

On the Parkway
Stable Affair
Kept
Stolen
Agitated
Love of my LIFE
Quickie in an Elevator,
GOING DOWN?
Into the Garden
The Book Case
The Other Women
Menage a WHAT?

E-Book Novellas

Children of Another Mother
Bikini's are Dangerous
Ghostly Love
Bikini's are Dangerous 2
Sapphic Surfer
The Rockhound
Bikini's are Dangerous 3
Bikini's are Dangerous 4
Bikini's are Dangerous 5
Mysterious Malice (Book 1)
Meticulous Malice (Book 2)
Mistaken Malice (Book 3)
Malicious Malice (Book 4)
Masterful Malice (Book 5)
Matrimonial Malice (Book 6)
Mourning Malice (Book 7)
Murderous Malice (Book 8)
Sapphic Cowgirl
Sapphic Cowboi
Mental Malice (Book 9)
Menacing Malice (Book 10)
Charming Thief

~Snake Island~
Charming Thief
~Diamonds are a Girls Best Friend~
Minor Malice (Book 11)
Morally Malice (Book 12)
Morose Malice (Book 13)
Melancholy Malice (Book 14)
Mad Malice (Book 15)
Macabre Malice (Book 16)
Marinating Malice (Book 17)
Macerating Malice (Book 18)
Minacious Malice (Book 19)
Sayyida
Meddlesome Malice (Book 20)
Meandering Malice (Book 21)
Maniacal Malice (Book 22)
The Northwood Lodge
Monitoring Malice (Book 23)
Marked Malice (Book 24)
Shanghaied
Outback Born

E-Book Novels

SHIPS *CompanionSHIP, FriendSHIP, RelationSHIP*
Erotica Volume 1
Long Distance Romance
Bikini's Are Dangerous
The Complete Series
Malice Masterpieces
The First Five Books
To Love a Shooting Star
Germanic
The Claim
Represented
Timed Romance
Blown Away
Blown Away *The Alternate Cover*
Malice Masterpieces 2
Books Six through Ten
The Journey Home
Out at the Inn
Anthology Volume 1
Lawyered

Malice Masterpieces 3
Books Eleven through Fifteen
Small Town Angel
Pirated Love
Doctored
Veil of Silence
Malice Masterpieces 4
Books Sixteen through Twenty
The Outsider
Pirated Heart
Recombinant Love
Survivors
Inn the Dog House
Flight
An Island Between Us

Vetted Series:
Vetted
Cavalcade (Prequel)
Pioneering (Prequel)
Vetted Further
Vetted Again

LARGE Print Novels

SHIPS CompanionSHIP, FriendSHIP, RelationSHIP
Erotica Volume 1
Long Distance Romance
Children of Another Mother
Bikini's Are Dangerous
The Complete Series

Malice Masterpieces
The First Five Books
To Love a Shooting Star
The Claim
Represented
Timed Romance

Audiobooks

Doctored
Sapphic Surfer
The Rockhound
Cavalcade

Pioneering
To Love A Shooting Star
Mysterious Malice

Videos

Biography of Books
Ships
Sapphic Surfer
Ghostly Love
Long Distance Romance
Germanic
Sensual Sapphic
Sapphic Cowgirl
Couples
Lie Next To Me

Sapphic Cowboi
Timed Romance
Readings (SHIPS)
Doctored
Veil of Silence
She's Coming (The Outsider short)
It's Coming (The Outsider short)
The Outsider
Vetted

K'ANNE MEINEL

OUTBACK BRED

ISBN-13: 978-1733661157

K'Anne Meinel is available for comments at KAnneMeinel@aim.com as well as on Facebook @ http://www.facebook.com/K.Anne.Meinel.Fan.Page, Google + @ https://plus.google.com/u/2/+KAnneMeinel, LinkedIn @ https://www.linkedin.com/in/k-anne-meinel-a026385a, or her blog @ http://kannemeinel.wordpress.com/ or on Twitter @ https://twitter.com/KAnneMeinel, or on her website @ www.kannemeinel.com if you would like to follow her to find out about stories and book's releases.

www.shadoepublishing.com

ShadoePublishing@gmail.com

Shadoe Publishing, LLC is a United States of America company

Cover by: K'Anne Meinel @ Shadoe Publishing
Edited by: Deb Amia, Grammar Queen grammarqueen.com

**Dedicated to anyone who
thinks I'm writing about them.
I am.**

OUTBACK BRED

CHAPTER ONE

Mel had come ashore wearing only the bedraggled clothes on her back. Sleeping, hidden on the rocks, she had to dry herself from the ocean water in the harbor before making her way into Sydney in the morning. She passed the pismire—the poor area—and many chain gangs, and she realized she better find clothing soon before they mistook her for an escaped convict instead of an escaped sailor. Shanghaied or not, she had deserted her ship. Finding a public outhouse, she gingerly pulled her pants down. She was afraid, not for herself but for what she had stored between her legs. The rolls of gold coins were disgusting from being bathed in her bodily fluids, including the blood she'd had to hide for those many months. The men had been too concerned about her pockets when they had rolled her, drugged her, and shanghaied her. They hadn't touched between her legs, or they would have found the fortune she carried there. On ship, she had rarely found time to change the coins' coverings, as she was forced to hastily use a bucket to poop and pee in when she found time alone. She knew her life would be in danger if they discovered her two secrets: the fortune and the fact that she was a woman. Her size and appearance had intimidated most men into believing she was a hard-working man. She extracted just one gold coin as she squatted over the hole and did her duty. There wasn't much to expel as she hadn't eaten in two days. She put the coin in her battered trousers, knowing she would be suspect if she held gold in her hand in any store. She headed away from the pismire, which was full of sharpsters, prostitutes, and people looking to take advantage of the unwary. Her size kept most people away, although she recognized the pickpocket children and kept her hand in her pocket, so the coin wouldn't disappear. Once in a better area, she made her way warily inside.

The establishment was like many common mercantile stores back in the states. There was a little of everything, and Mel began to look for trousers that would fit her.

"May I help you?" the man behind the counter said haughtily after a few customers backed away from the sailor, who wore no shoes, had dirty feet, and looked worse for wear in disreputable and well-worn clothing. She knew she probably smelled too.

"Yes, I need a whole new outfit," Mel said cheerfully, trying to keep her voice low and indistinguishable as she had trained herself so long ago.

"Can you afford to pay for that?" he asked disdainfully, looking the man before him up and down and not finding him pleasing to the eye. He also recognized the American accent.

"Yep, I was paid today and thought I'd treat myself. You got any ready-made shirts?" Mel asked, hoping the man wouldn't report her, but she knew news of an American sailor would spread quickly in any town, and she wanted to be dressed and ready before the authorities came.

There was quite a stack of clothing and other things Mel felt she needed, but the shoes would hurt her feet after many months of going barefoot on the deck of a ship, and she knew she would have to get used to wearing footwear again. Shoes alone were not going to do it; she needed boots and that meant a bootmaker.

"How much do I owe you for all this?" she asked as they finished up her business and the man's eyebrows nearly disappeared into his bangs when she pulled out the one gold coin she had in her pocket. It more than paid for the supplies she was buying, and she began to stuff things in the satchel and saddle bags she had put on the counter as the man got her change. "Aren't you a little short?" she asked him when he returned.

"Short?" he asked, and when he hesitated, they both knew he was trying to get away with something.

She quoted the price for the supplies she had asked him about, the gold coin's value, and easily subtracted in her head to arrive at the sum she should receive. She was being shorted quite a bit by the amount he had given her.

"You aren't allowing for the difference between American money and coin of the realm," he tried, but Mel wasn't an idiot. Gold was gold.

"Look, I can call the constable in here, and he can hear both sides of our story, but stories of you cheating me will get around pretty quickly, if I do that," she pointed out. The man gulped. Mel's size hadn't gone unnoticed either.

"And how do I know you haven't deserted your ship and stolen that coin?" he asked in return.

"Who do you think the constable will believe when he hears my story and what you tried to do?" she bluffed. Her heart was beating so hard she could hear it pounding against her skull. He was right. They wouldn't believe her, and she'd probably be arrested.

He quickly came up with the rest of her change, and she swiftly folded it into her pocket. "You got somewhere I can change into my new clothes?" she asked as though nothing had transpired between them.

Mel changed out of the sailor clothes, using some cloth she had bought from the man to rewrap her breasts under the new men's shirt she eagerly buttoned up. It was long enough that she could wear it as a nightshirt, and she knew many men did just that. She fished out her money from her front pants' pocket. She needed to buy a purse or a wallet to keep her money in. She didn't want to tempt the pickpockets. She left the rolls of coins between her legs, used to them being there after all this time, but she knew she would have to deposit some of them, and soon.

She gingerly pulled the new socks on over her dirty feet, cringing and then stuffing her feet in the stiff, new shoes. Still, when all was said and done, she felt better in the new, clean clothes. She put a belt around her middle, a knife hanging from its fitted leather scabbard. She picked up her satchel after stuffing her old sailor's clothes deep within it and slung her now full saddle bags over her broad shoulder. She nodded stiffly to the shopkeeper, who was already helping other

customers and made her way gingerly out of the store and into the sunshine. The shoes felt unfamiliar on her feet. She headed for a barbershop, getting her now overly long and clubbed hair cut into a decent man's haircut. She had the barber leave it a bit longer than she liked; she didn't want it left so short that she looked like a hick…or a convict. She flipped a coin to the barber when he was done. He'd given her the name of a good bootmaker and directed her on her way.

At the bootmaker's, she stood as the man measured her in her socks for boots, telling him what she was looking for, and he promised to deliver them in a week. She headed for a hotel, one well away from the pismire but not so nice that only nabobs would stay there. She paid for her room, ordered a bath for that evening, and headed out again, this time without her saddlebags or satchel. She headed for another store, looking for more ready-made clothing and supplies. She also found a tailor and ordered a nice suit—nothing too dapper but better than the casual clothes she was wearing. Because she would allow no measuring or fitting, it didn't look quite right on her. Still, she was pleased with the result. She'd purchased some ready-made miners' pants, something they were calling jeans back in the states, that were made of a hardy dungaree material that didn't rip easily. She was making contacts, and Mel Lawrence was now a nicely dressed young man. But when she visited a dress shop to purchase a ready-made dress, she ran into problems.

"I'm sorry, we only dress women," the woman began snootily.

"And I assure you, madam, I am a woman," Mel told her just as snobbily, drawing on her upbringing and all the women who had treated her badly for so long just because she was not an attractive woman. It felt good to allow her normal voice to be heard after so long. "I need a day dress to conduct some business, and I want to look nice. I can't always be wearing this," she indicated the men's trousers and shirt she was now wearing. At least they were clean, even if her body wasn't. She could still feel the salt on her skin and the dirt in her pores. It was so easy to hide in plain sight since she could carry off the looks of both an unattractive woman and an average-looking man.

"Well, I never–" the woman began.

"Well, maybe you should," Mel finished for her. "Look, lady. My money is as good as the next woman's, and I pay on time when the work is finished. I don't want anything too frilly or too fancy, just stylish and acceptable to conduct business in."

It was the promise of being paid on time that made the dressmaker concede. So many of her customers used credit, and it could sometimes be years before she saw a farthing. "Half up front," she found herself saying.

"I'll give you that, but you must work quickly," Mel countered, pulling the wallet she had purchased at the second store from her front pocket and extracting a couple bills. She didn't know the exchange rate, but she knew the few bills she gave the woman were more than enough.

"Let's get you measured," the woman said as she scooped up the cash and tucked it in her ample bosom. "If you would, please come in the back." She wanted to hide this unsightly woman in case anyone mistakenly thought she was dressing men these days. Business was off due to one of those eternal slumps in the market, so she really couldn't afford to turn away any cash business.

Mel had had countless fittings in the past. Her father had always wanted his little girl to look her best, but he could never completely

cover up the homely girl he had fathered. Still, he had loved her regardless of her looks, unaware or oblivious of the shunning of other girls and later, women. Instead, he had taught her useful life skills, instilling pride in her and teaching her to stand on her own two feet. This fitting was a little odd, mostly because she stood there in her trousers, shirtless, and wearing no undergarment. The wrappings hid her assets as the seamstress measured and looked away from her customer.

"I don't want frills or corsets or any of that frippery," she told the dressmaker. "I want something stylish and classy, and don't think you can pass just anything off on me. You've been paid half, and if you get this done in a week, I'll give you your payment in full."

The woman nodded, writing down her customer's measurements on a piece of paper and eventually, allowing Mel to put her shirt back on. "I've got a couple designs I can show you," the woman offered reluctantly, but her had attitude had thawed with the down payment.

Mel finished buttoning up her shirt and tucked it into the back of her pants. She could feel the coins between her legs, not for the first time, but suddenly, she was feeling conspicuous about them in the presence of this other woman. The woman was attractive now that she wasn't so ruffled up about a man coming into her shop. Mel could feel the attraction but knew better than to act on it. It was always better when the other woman made the first move, and she was quite certain this seamstress was not attracted to women.

The sketches that the woman presented showed her that fashion had changed in the many months she had been away from New York, yet some of them were still behind what she had seen on the women back there. She pointed to a few things, making suggestions, and surprising the seamstress with her knowledge of fashion. Mel's suggestions were doable, and the seamstress would update the designs, incorporating several of the ideas Mel had asked for.

"Have they really gone that far in New York?" she asked, surprised and delighted by Mel's suggestions. New York sounded like Paris or Milan to her. Here in Sydney, she was months behind fashions in London, when or if she could obtain current design sketches.

Mel left the seamstress in a terrific mood. It was the first time in a long time that a woman had appreciated her as a woman, not sexually but as one woman to another. She'd enjoyed talking fashion for the first time in years. Ultimately, the woman hadn't judged her once she got past Mel's looks, and talking fashion had brought back memories of a time when she had actually enjoyed being a girl, before she had grown into a masculine woman and had been judged by other women on the marriage mart. They had been so cruel to the awkward, unattractive teen, all in the name of finding a husband and weeding out the competition.

Mel returned to her hotel. It had been quite the day, and she was pleased to see the tub was already set up in her room. The clerk at the front desk had seen her enter, and within a few minutes, boys were arriving with steaming buckets of water and pouring them into the tub until it was half full. Locking the door, Mel propped a chair up against it before closing the window shades and undressing. It felt heavenly to immerse her body in the warm water and lather up using the soap she had purchased that day. It was a sandalwood that teased her senses and wasn't too girly. It made her feel clean for the first time in months. The rainstorms she had lived through on board the boat had nothing over a good soak in the tub. The saltwater in the bay had gotten into

every pore, and she was pleased to soak it away. Finally, she submerged her head and scrubbed at it with the soap, creating a foam and feeling truly clean for the first time in months. Emerging from the tub, she grabbed the towel and briskly rubbed herself dry. Using clean wraps, she bound her breasts, slipped on summer underwear with a flap like some men wore, and pulled on socks and some black, ready-made trousers. Carefully, she put on one of the finer white shirts she had purchased, using cuff links on the sleeves, which required her full concentration since she had no one to help her put them on. Finally, she donned a black vest, buttoned it down, and covered it with a matching jacket. Looking in the mirror, she slicked her hair back with her fingers, realizing she had not purchased a comb or brush and knowing she would have to rectify that. The clothes, while not tailored, didn't look half bad. The creases in the white shirt should have been ironed out, and the vest was a little tight across her bound breasts, but the coat covered these faults, making her look robust and fine.

The stylish young man went down to dine, stopping by the front desk to ask them to remove the dirty bath water and tub, then went on to one of the city's nicer restaurants. Several people looked curiously at Mel, wondering who the Yank was and what *his* business was in Sydney. In a voice carefully modulated to neither reveal nor define her as a woman since she was dressed as a man, Mel asked for a table and began to peruse the menu selections. In the end, she ordered steak, potatoes, and a fine wine. She'd read that Australia was producing its own wines and wanted to try one. She'd tried American wines on both coasts, even French and other European wines over the years as she traveled with her father, and she was pleased that the Australian wine was delicious, rich, and a perfect accompaniment to her meal. She was surprised she couldn't eat the whole meal but realized after months at sea her stomach had probably shrunk.

"You're a Yank, aren't ya?" a voice addressed her from a neighboring table. Mel looked up at the man and nodded, wondering if she could have dined in peace if she hadn't opened her mouth to order. "What brings you to Australia?" She realized he was just making conversation since he was also dining alone.

"I'm thinking of investing down here and came to get the lay of the land, as it were," she lied convincingly. Catching a boat back to San Francisco so soon after her previous voyage didn't appeal to her now, but she was in a new country, and she realized she could start over where no one knew her…she could essentially disappear, if she wanted.

"There's plenty to be had with the right coin in the right wallet," he quipped knowingly with a wink. The clothes she was wearing didn't tell him if she had money or not, but the manners Mel displayed, even unconsciously, showed her fine upbringing.

"Ah, that is what I figured," she answered, deliberately sounding American since she knew that would be expected. She also didn't want to encourage him since sharpsters existed in all levels of society, and if it were known that she had money, they wouldn't hesitate to try and do her out of that money. Still, it was nice to talk to someone since most times she chose to be alone, especially after what she had just escaped from. The close confines of the ship hadn't been to her liking, and her fear of being found out had not allowed her to relax. Any superfluous flesh on her frame was now gone, which she had noted in the dressmaker's store. She chatted with the man a while, wishing she had something to do with her hands as she had finished as much of her meal as she was going to finish. She noted that several men had lit cigars or

pipes, and that surprised her, until she realized no ladies were present to object. She paid for her meal when the waiter presented her with the check, using the billfold she had purchased earlier in the day. It wasn't packed full of bills, but after having cashed her gold piece earlier, she now had the proper bills to use. She knew that pulling out a gold piece would only draw unwanted attention, and she wanted to avoid that. Bidding the gentlemen at the next table a good night, she exited into the night air, breathing in her freedom like a tonic. She must decide what she wanted to do.

Returning to America did not appeal in the least. She was also afraid to go near the docks in case any of her shipmates were looking for her. She didn't wish them any further ill will, and she hoped by moving to a different section of Sydney and changing her clothes, they wouldn't find her. A sailor who abandons his ship is due some severe punishment, but she knew that the type of men she had left behind wouldn't hesitate to shanghai her again, and she never wanted to repeat that experience. She was certain if she was taken back to *that* ship, they would make her life miserable, working her as a slave until they ultimately killed her.

What did she want to do in Australia?

She sat down on the bench outside her hotel contemplating and watching the evening shadows and the few people out and about. She had enjoyed working with cattle before she was shanghaied, but she didn't think she wanted a cattle ranch of her own. She was already fed up with people and wanted some alone time. Perhaps, she should head for the Outback that she had heard so much of, but she didn't know enough about it to make an informed decision either way. She could live on her funds indefinitely, and in the dress she intended to wear to the bank next week, she would make arrangements for some of Melissa Lawrence's funds from America to be transferred to a new bank account here. Her signature and appearance would make an impression, and in the future, Mel Lawrence and *his* looks and appearance wouldn't matter once she was established. The coin she had with her would give her an immediate and indefinite cushion until they verified the transfer of funds from one country to another. She wouldn't take all the Lawrence funds out of America. She hadn't taken them out of Europe either, clinging to her father's advice of diversification. Well, Australia was just as diverse as America, and she would see what she could find here. Maybe she would find her future?

CHAPTER TWO

Mel spent her days walking about Sydney, getting a feel for the large city that seemed to be bursting at the seams. Dressed as a gentleman of means while avoiding being too showy or dapper, she was breaking in the hated shoes while waiting until her boots could be finished. She went to coffee houses to listen to men talk for hours, a place where women were not allowed and which supplied her with plenty of gossip, debates, and a few insights into the markets down here. She learned that sheep, not cattle, were the main industry in the Outback, although there were plenty of cattle ranches too. They didn't call them ranches here; they were called stations. There was also plenty of shipping here as Sydney was strategically located for whalers and commerce, and it was becoming an important port.

She picked up a nice brush and comb set. It wasn't too feminine but would last her a long time. At the same time, she picked up a couple pipes, and after much contemplation, she bought different tobaccos to try, remembering the fragrances her father favored and bringing back fond memories of growing up around those aromas. Her own attempts at smoking were dismal, leaving her feeling slightly nauseous. She learned that just leaving the pipe smoldering after a meal was best, the tobacco leaves giving off delicious scents. She sucked on the stem from time to time to keep the leaves of tobacco lit and held the smoke in her mouth to release it slowly. Smoking helped to complete her *look* of a young man about town, or so she thought.

The day her boots were ready, she stomped into them, and the fine fit pleased her so much that she impulsively ordered a second pair, paying the bootmaker on the spot for the first pair. They felt a bit snug since the leather wasn't worn in, but for the first time in months, she felt fine. Strangely, that was the day her dress was ready as well. Trying it on in the dressmaker's shop, she was pleased with the results. She was also pleased by the fact that she could dress herself without the help of a maid. The dressmaker had incorporated her ideas, making the dress stylish without all the frippery that usually accompanied a fashionable dress. She had also included a matching cape that enhanced the beauty of the dress, and the hood could be utilized to hide Mel's short hair. Undressing at the store, she overheard the woman complaining to someone that she was simply running out of room and couldn't hire more seamstresses due to the lack of space. Mel had seen two seamstresses who were ignoring her in their desire to sew as quickly as possible and not earn the ire of their taskmistress.

"Mrs. Waters, your work is impeccable," she informed the woman as she promptly paid the rest of her bill. She was dressed casually in her men's suit with no cravat and carried the dress over her arm.

"I'm so glad you are pleased," she said modestly, counting out the money that Mel paid her. "I will box that up for you," she said, reaching for the dress. She noted the suit that was obviously not designed for Mel's frame. As she boxed up the dress, she mentioned in a low voice, so her seamstresses would not overhear, "I could design you a couple of suits," she nodded towards the one Mel was wearing, "that would look like they were made especially for you and not so," she wrinkled her nose a little in her snobbishness as she searched for the right word, "…ill-fitting?"

Mel had been pleased with the suit she purchased and put together from two different stores. She thought she looked fine in it and had worn it every day for a week, so at first, she was insulted by the dressmaker's comment. Then, she realized the woman understood her unique situation and nodded. "Do you have the material?"

The woman shook her head. "I could have some samples here by tomorrow, if you are interested?" She was hoping to get more business from this unusual customer, who paid so punctually.

"That would be fine. I would want at least two suits that fit me," Mel decided. "I will be in tomorrow to look at what you have."

"I will see you then," the woman smiled as she handed Mel the box, thinking that while this was an unattractive woman, she didn't look too bad in her male attire. She would, of course, make her look better in her own creations.

Mel felt better knowing the woman's incentive was her money and not the challenge of dressing her. She took her box back to the hotel, changed out of her men's suit, which she still thought looked just fine, and got into the new dress. The woman standing before her in the mirror would still never be accepted into polite society, here or elsewhere. She was just too blunt looking, too masculine, too big. She had accepted that many years ago, and while her father had said he loved her as she was, she knew he was disappointed that she hadn't married and given him a grandchild to dangle on his knee. She shrugged. She had business to attend to, and she put her cape on to cover her dress and hide her hair, tying it under her chin. She slipped one of the rolls of gold coins in her new reticule along with her room key and the small gun she had also acquired. She smiled as she remembered purchasing the gun and asking not for a cap and ball pistol but one that would fire five bullets before needing to be reloaded. She was seen leaving Mel Lawrence's room before noon by one of the hotel staff, and unbeknownst to her at the time, this sighting enhanced the young man's reputation.

The bank she had chosen had branches in London as well as here in Sydney. The Bank of England was backed by the government and reasonably solvent. Mel had wanted to avoid an investment bank that would be vulnerable to depositors and men who handled such investments without fear of government interference. Those types of banks were not where she wanted her funds to be handled. Even her diversification in the States and in Europe spread her funds between government banks and the type of bank she was avoiding now. With governments rising and falling, and banks subject to crashes, by having her funds spread out she should be able to avoid ever being totally wiped out by any major crash. At least, that was what her father had taught her as he explained his own thoughts on the subject to his only

heir. The fact that he held no notions that a woman couldn't handle her own affairs or understand international banking had helped her become the woman she was.

Keeping her hood up and her face visible, she was able to open an account. Using the roll of gold coins to fund the account and provide her with monies to invest in things she might be interested in here in Australia ensured that she was behaving responsibly. She had washed out all the coins and separated out the two rolls. She still worried about the roll she had hidden beneath the floorboard she pried up in her hotel room; however, she wouldn't put all her ready funds in a foreign bank. She waited as the bank clerk drew up several drafts of the letter that would go to her bank in New York to arrange for further funds to be transferred here to Sydney. Signing them as Melissa Lawrence, she realized they were surprised that a woman was making these arrangements without the assistance of a man. She didn't say anything about how she had come to be in Australia and what she would be doing with her funds. Despite the chatty bank manager, who tried to draw her out, her monosyllable answers managed to discourage any further conversation.

"Miss Lawrence are you sure you don't need your father or an uncle or brother to help you with this?" the bank manager asked, condescendingly. Mel stared him down, not answering the rude question. When he repeated this type of question throughout their transaction, she finally spoke up.

"Would it be better, Mr. Hathaway, if the Lawrence funds," she indicated the letter to the bank in New York that she had signed, "were put in another institution here in Australia?"

He hastily backed down as he didn't want to lose her business. She had deposited a large amount of money, and they were surprised it was all in gold since gold was hard to come by here in Australia. While it was unusual for a woman to oversee such funds, he wouldn't question her further. He would, however, continue to monitor her account as he was certain there was something afoot here. She would not have access to the funds she was transferring from the Americas for several months, but the money from the gold ensured that she had plenty of ready money to do with as she saw fit.

Returning from the bank, Mel gladly replaced her fine dress in its box along with the cloak and reticule. She wasn't sure she would ever need them again, but she wanted them close by just in case. One never knew. She dressed once again in her suit, still a little stung by Mrs. Waters' opinion of it but looking forward to seeing the samples she had promised. That led her to think about the small seamstress' store. The woman obviously knew what she was doing but didn't have the business sense to expand. If she was busy enough to employ two other seamstresses full-time, what could she do if she had the wherewithal to employ four or more? How about the room? Mel contemplated that as she stomped back into her boots, putting the hated and ill-fitting shoes aside once again. She liked the boots, and while they hurt a little, she knew in time, they would fit perfectly.

Mel sat in a coffeehouse, aware that the men who frequented them gave out far too much information as they discussed their investments, speculated on others' investments, and wasted time before going back to their offices. She saw the coffee houses as a gathering place for men, young and old, to gossip. She bought a newspaper, reading it from front to back as she listened to them talk. She did this several

times a week, frequenting different coffee houses each time and establishing her presence there, so she became a familiar sight. Her status as a Yank ensured speculation about her presence, but since she was accepted as a man, they talked freely around her as she bought an occasional drink for her new friends. She even bought stock in a few shipping ventures, ones she had heard gossip about and was certain would net results after doing her own research.

She found that the stocks in shipping could be quite lucrative. She didn't invest heavily, but as shippers of goods couldn't afford to buy their own stocks, they often took on investors, who expected a return on their investment. The return varied by the different merchandise stored in these great ships, and the fact that Mel could talk with a reasonable amount of knowledge about ships garnered her information they didn't even realize they were releasing.

Mel was restless while waiting for her funds to arrive from America. The months of idleness and visiting coffee houses eventually bored her to tears. Instead of just sitting about, she kept herself active by renting a horse and using it to go farther afield in this great city as she explored and learned more about it. She found a liking for taking a road out to a town called Parramatta. Her horse clomped on the cobblestone streets of Sydney until she got farther out and onto the dirt roads. The cobblestones reminded her of those she had seen in England as well as New England. She could see that it took several hours for a wagon to go from Sydney into Parramatta. She took Parramatta Road out past the brickyard and market. Farmers at the market discussed the relative merits of sheep, cattle, pigs, and horses, and she ate it up, enjoying the easy talk and learning a lot from them and their interest in her as a Yank. There was a tang in the air from the trees. Someone

explained they were called Eucalyptus trees. She had never seen trees where the bark peeled from the base. Apparently, there were many different varieties of trees in this new land, and she was learning all about them. Even more fascinating were the various birds she saw in their branches. There seemed to be brightly colored birds like a rainbow, and they looked nothing like any birds she had seen before in her life. She would learn that they were rosellas, lorikeets, and crested pigeons, all names she had never heard before but which fascinated her. She loved seeing the church spires that were prevalent in the town when she headed back.

The two suits that Mrs. Waters made for her fit wonderfully and ensured that she was always nicely dressed in the coffee houses. However, when she went farther afield, she found that this attire was looked on with suspicion in the taverns, so she acquired a loose-fitting shirt and a few pairs of common trousers that tucked nicely into the boots she'd had made. A western hat, called a stockman's hat and made in the style the Australians seemed to favor, along with a matching leather jacket completed the look and calmed the natives, who seemed unnaturally suspicious of her American accent. Still, foreigners were pouring into Sydney and settling the farthest reaches of the colony and growing city.

It was in one of the taverns off Parramatta Road that she learned more about the Outback while listening to fascinating tales of dark people, some savages, who roamed this vast wasteland. Others, closer to the city, talked about the fact that farmland and grazing land were to be had for the taking. One farmer Mel spoke with at length talked about how quickly they were running out of room here in this part of

Australia. He was thinking of selling out and going inland, but his wife didn't want to lose civilization and was frankly afraid of the unknown.

Mel traveled as far as the town of Parramatta and gazed at the still far-off Blue Mountains. They didn't remind her of the mountains in Kentucky and certainly weren't as high as the Rockies in Colorado, but they had their own appeal, and she could feel them drawing her. Was this where her destiny lay? She knew staying in Sydney indefinitely was not what she wanted. She felt she had already wasted a lot of time there and wanted to be doing something else.

It was in Parramatta that she talked with grazers, ranchers with small properties, and she learned that the sheep trade was also much more prevalent in this part of the country than cattle. While she had no experience with sheep, she had enjoyed her time herding cattle despite the fact it had led to her own downfall and getting shanghaied.

"Why don't you come out to my section? I'll teach ya what ya need to know," one of the grazers offered helpfully. "We're always shorthanded. We need stockmen, and it's nearly time for our lambing season."

Mel carefully considered the offer, knowing she had nothing better to do and anxious to fill the many hours she wasted each day. Her money would still take months to arrive from America and exploring the city had lost its appeal. Agreeing to help in exchange for what the man was willing to teach her, she learned where his station was and returned to the city to pack her bags.

"We'll miss having you here, Mr. Lawrence," the clerk at the desk told her when she checked out. "If any mail comes for you, where do you want it sent?" he asked by way of finding out where this long-time hotel guest would be going.

"Have it sent in care of the Parramatta post office," she answered without giving away too much. Carrying her two bags with her saddlebags over her shoulder and wearing her jacket and hat, she made her way to the stockyards to buy a horse.

While looking over the selection of horses for carriages—from ones that would be fine in the city and were similar to the ones she had rented to ones that were bulky, stocky, and good for pulling wagons or plows—she noticed some very shaggy horses, which reminded her of the Mustangs she had seen in America. Inquiring about them with her American accent, the man very condescendingly explained that these were Outback horses and some of them had been wild.

"They are called Brumbies," he explained, assuming this Yank knew nothing about horses.

Mel watched the horses. They seemed a little dispirited in the corral, their longer, shaggier hair more suited to colder climates than here on the coast. While it had become colder, necessitating wearing warmer clothes, it wasn't nearly as cold as some of the places where she had lived in America. Still, it was late spring here in Australia, and the people she had spoken with claimed it got almost stifling hot here.

Choosing from among the Brumbies, she picked a strong-looking gelding, who had an almost dun color to his coat but more Palomino that appealed to her. His gait was strong, he was cocky and confident, and he showed off for her. He sniffed at her thoroughly as they became acquainted, and she bought the gear including an Australian saddle. She noted it had no pommel like the saddles in the western United States. She wondered at that but didn't question it since the man already assumed she was an unknowing Yank. Saddling up the horse,

she tied on her saddlebags and two duffel bags before mounting up and heading towards Parramatta.

The section was larger than she had been led to believe but still remote. As she looked at the strange vegetation, the eucalyptus trees and different plants and grasses, she marveled at the new country she was making her own. As she pulled her horse up in the yard, a couple of men looked at her curiously. Foster, the man she had met, came out of a low-slung house and greeted her.

"I see you found us," he stated, smiling to show he was pleased that she had shown up on the station.

"Yes, willing and able to work," she said with a smile as she got down.

"That's a fine-lookin' horse ya got there," he said admiringly. "Looks like a Brumby."

"You got a fine eye, and he is a Brumby, at least according to the horse dealer."

"You can put him up over there," he nodded towards what was obviously a barn, although it didn't look like the ones she was used to seeing in America. It was more of a large, low, and ramshackle shed. "The barracks are over there for your gear." He nodded again to another building a few yards down from the barn where smoke was already rising from the smoke pipe. This building had also been carelessly put together. "Dinner is at sundown, and we're up at four."

She nodded to acknowledge the information and led the horse to the barn. She unpacked her belongings and put her saddle up before letting him out into the corral where he began to become acquainted with the horses there. She carried her two duffels and saddle bags into the barracks, saw an empty lower bunk a ways from the others in a corner, and put her things on it. She saw a fire was already going in the stove and went outside to meet a couple of the men.

"This is Bart, and this is Calvin," Foster said as he introduced the men. "Bart is our cook, and Calvin does odd chores."

Bart had a gimpy leg that she would later learn was caused by a kick from a horse at some point in his life. He had worked from job to job until Foster gave him the permanent job as cook on his station. She shook Calvin's hand, which seemed to surprise the aboriginal man, but he showed his pleasure with a smile, his even, very white teeth in stark contrast against his dark skin. She returned the smile. The men started talking about sheep, and she listened avidly, contributing little since she didn't know much. She saw that the shearing shed, the corrals, the runways, and everything to do with sheep were in much better shape than anything else on the station.

She met more of the men at dinner and found out there were many more working in the paddocks.

"I've divided my place into four sections. We can pretty much keep the sheep out there indefinitely, so they don't graze the paddocks down too much. A sheep will eat down to the roots if it doesn't have fresh graze," Foster explained, and the other men contributed their own views on this as well as sharing what they had seen and experienced on other stations.

The learning began from that first conversation, and Mel was an avid pupil. She found one of the men rifling through her belongings that first night and confronted him. "We got a dandy here boys, a Yank," he said gleefully, holding up one of her suits.

"And you are a thief," she stated as she started forward, punching the man and grabbing at her suit at the same time. Her punch landed

but only because the man hadn't expected her to attack so suddenly while he was laughing at her and her clothes. The suit was ripped out of his hands, and he was propelled backwards into the wall of the barracks. He bounced back up, shocked that she had struck him. "That's my stuff, mate," she said sarcastically, deliberately using an Australian term to taunt him. He came at her then, angered by both her punch and her taunt. She dropped the suit on her bunk and threw him aside in a rolling hip maneuver that put him off balance and propelled him forward into another set of bunks. His head struck painfully, stunning him. The others, who had either been on their own bunks or had come in after Mel, stared in surprise at how easily Mel handled the man. She picked him up by the back of his shirt and asked, "Are you done?"

He shook his head, and she began to propel him towards the door of the barracks, keeping him off balance. One of the men held the door wide when he saw her direction. She threw the man across the small porch, kicking him in the ass as a bonus. Her nearly new boots must have really hurt as she propelled him far out into the dirt of the yard, face first.

"What?" Foster asked as he came out of the chow hall and the men exited the barracks to watch the unexpected fight.

"Are you done?" Mel asked the man again. He shook his head once more. "You shaking your head to clear it, or are you not done?" she asked.

"I'll get you for–" he began and pulled a knife as he lunged up.

Mel slapped the knife out of line with her body and then kicked the man again, this time in the belly as he had turned over to pull his knife. For added measure, she stepped hard on his arm as he went down and

yanked the knife out of his hand before throwing it away. "Are you done yet?" she asked him for the third time, her eyes glittering dangerously.

This time, the pain in his stomach and arm were enough to make him vomit the fine dinner he had just eaten, and he nodded.

Mel immediately got off his arm and offered him a hand up by his good arm. He looked at her hand suspiciously as she held it there. Finally, he took it gingerly and allowed her to pull him up. It took a moment for him to steady himself. "You'll stay away from my stuff. I don't want to have to repeat this, or next time, I'll kill you," she told him conversationally. She heard a couple gasps from the onlookers, but the man nodded as he held his middle with his good arm while bending forward slightly. Mel turned away and looked at the men watching, then went back into the bunkhouse to arrange her things. She knew where her money was hidden and knew the man would not have found it, but the packed dress might have puzzled anyone who found it. Still, she didn't like that someone had gone through her things.

CHAPTER THREE

The real work started the next morning. Mel woke as soon as she heard movement from the other men. She pulled on her trousers from the previous day and tucked in the buttoned shirt she had slept in. She made her way to the outhouse; a couple of the men not bothering and just peeing wherever they stood as they woke up in the early morning cold. Used to such habits and knowing how to avoid the situation, Mel closed the door on the outhouse and quickly pulled her pants down after making sure there were no leavings or animals on the seat. She'd heard they had some of the deadliest snakes in the world here in Australia, and she didn't want anyone playing tricks on her. It was such a relief just to be able to use the necessary without worrying about the rolls of gold coins anymore; it had completely changed her stride when the rolls were no longer between her legs.

Breakfast was rushed, and Mel went to the barn and got her horse saddled as she gathered her hat and jacket and mounted up. Foster led her out to one of the paddocks, talking about the sheep.

"I have several varieties I'm cross-breeding. I'm hoping to get a higher yield of wool. I wish I could afford Merinos. Those seem to be some of the best I've seen, but few people can afford to raise them, much less have them imported."

Mel nodded, wondering if Foster would bring up the fight of the previous night, but she wasn't going to start that conversation. She was listening avidly because the more she thought about it, the more she thought she wanted to get a grazing license and possibly establish her own station. She had heard that the Outback was lonely, but she just wanted to get free of people and have her own space. The more time she spent in the city amongst people, the more she wanted to be alone. After her experience on the ship, she wanted nothing to do with men and their ways, and the only woman she had met that would have sparked an interest in her didn't realize the attraction, so it was obvious she wasn't a woman lover.

"Let's show you how to control the dogs," Foster said as he introduced her to one of his sheep herders and his apprentice. "Why don't you two go into the station house and take the day off?" he suggested. He didn't have to ask the man and boy twice. They took off on their horses with no delay.

Foster explained how the commands to the dogs worked. "I'm breeding more of these," he indicated the dogs. "I hope to find a standard for the breed with the crosses I've found that were imported from England."

He talked knowledgeably about all aspects of the breeding of both sheep and dogs, and he even knew a bit about cattle, a conversation Mel could contribute to. Then his talk turned to horses. The education Mel was getting seemed to be well-rounded, and she appreciated it when he taught her various things.

"So, you've herded cattle then?" Foster commented, having wondered about this Yank, who seemed so keen on learning about sheep. Even the breeding and raising of dogs seemed to hold the man's attention, but he didn't tell very much about himself and how he had come to be in Australia.

"Yes, I worked on a few ranches for a while, and then I took a herd across the northern desert of Nevada to the mining camps before I went on to San Francisco." Mel didn't tell him anymore since it was outside San Francisco where she had been given the knockout drops that enabled them to shanghai her and she woke up on that fateful ship. Now, here in Australia, she was going to start over.

Foster showed her all the basic commands, calling in four of the dogs, who were spaced around the flock of sheep. He explained that they had been taught not to bark, so they wouldn't scare the sheep. He demonstrated how to signal the dogs using a combination of whistles, hand gestures, and commands.

At first, it was laughable when Mel tried to get the dogs to do what she wanted. They were confused because she was unsure of herself and her gestures lacked confidence. When she wanted them to go one way but they were sent another, she swore aloud. They heard her swearing and thought she was giving another command. Foster stood back and let her make mistakes over and over. Slowly, she began to get a feel for it. The dogs, she was sure, were laughing at her as they panted.

The intelligence in their eyes was amazing to see, and they were eager to please and eager to work. This surprised her as she hadn't ever worked with dogs before. Some were black and white, some were brown and white, and others were various shades in between. There were some with a brindle color to their coats that appealed to her. Their bodies were compact, and they were not much smaller than the different sheep in the flock. She practiced for hours until Foster clapped his hand on her shoulder and gave her a compliment.

"I've seen it take days for someone to learn what took you only hours. You are catching on faster than I would have believed. Let's take this lot into the station. They are due to give birth, and I always like to have at least one of my flocks in for this. Let's see how you do and if you remember how to get back to the station. It can get confusing out here." He gestured to the paddock where the sheep were fairly contained, which went on for a ways.

At first, Mel *was* confused. Everything looked the same, and she hadn't watched very closely while she had been practicing with the dogs for all these hours. Then, she began to sort herself out. She realized that the sun still set in the west, and that gave her one direction. She recalled Foster saying this was his northwest paddock, so the home paddock must be southeast, and with this knowledge she got up on her horse and began to signal the dogs, feeling more confident than she had in hours. Foster watched, and when she had gotten far enough ahead of him, he smiled because she had figured it out very quickly.

Foster circled wide, so he could open the gates for the sheep, and after they went through, he closed them as they headed back. It was late afternoon and nearly time for dinner when they got the sheep in the

home paddocks. After talking sheep with Foster some more and learning the different reasons for different breeds, she commanded the dogs to follow her, and Foster showed her how to feed them. The four dogs were ravenously hungry, and while they fed the dogs, he explained why they kept so many wethers (castrated sheep), what were their purposes, and how long a carcass could last a man before it became too gamy to eat.

"You want to keep everything well covered," he said, showing her how to cover the carcass with a bag, "or the flies will lay their eggs." There were flies, lots of them, and they were pesky things that she had learned to ignore out here.

Mel was filthy and washed up at the trough outside the barracks. She had a fine coat of dust on her clothes and easily swatted herself down with her hat. She'd taken her duffel bags into the loft of the barn while others were at breakfast that morning and hidden them deep in the hay, leaving only her saddle bags for anyone with too much curiosity about her. She pulled a shirt out of one of the bags and quickly changed into it, so she would have on a clean shirt for dinner. She was feeling a need to "dress up" as she had in the days of old, which felt like almost a lifetime ago. She quickly washed the shirt she had worn that day, laying it out, so it would dry in the hot air.

Dinner was fresh beef. They killed an animal that had gotten hung up in some fence and ripped the hell out of his hide before he could be freed. He'd been too torn up to survive, so they had butchered the poor beast and put it out of its misery. That meant fresh meat, and the cook had been busy putting it all up and making their meal.

"There'll be plenty of stew next week as they give birth," he promised the men, nodding towards the sheep, and they cheered, looking forward to their meals since they worked so hard.

"I think I saw our first lamb," one of the men commented.

"Not in the flock we brought in," Foster commented as he reached for some bread to sop up the juices on his plate, talking with food in his mouth.

"No, I was out mending the fence in the eastern paddock where this guy got his horns locked," he indicated the meat they were eating. "I thought I saw a lamb and its mama."

"Someone must ride out and check. We didn't breed those ewes until last, and if a ram got in there early, I want to know how," Foster told the men.

"What happens if the ram got in there early?" Mel asked, hoping it didn't sound like a stupid question.

"Then our work is early and unexpected," Foster replied, sounding angry. "We send the rams in with each flock, so the births are spaced out days apart and not all at once. They're randy buggers and do a good job but if they somehow got in a flock early, we are going to be too busy."

The others agreed as they stuffed as much food as possible in their faces as quickly as they could. Mel, a hearty eater herself, was amazed at the vast quantities of bread and beef they consumed. The vegetables weren't ignored either, and the men belched and farted with impunity. It always amazed her how men behaved when they didn't know a woman was around, although some behaved the same way with women around, now that she thought about it.

Over the next few days, Mel learned more about how to take care of sheep, also learning to control the dogs better. Foster eventually left her alone with one of his flocks in a pasture. At first, she was terrified to be out there unaided with so much responsibility. At the same time, she welcomed the silence, although it was never completely quiet. The animals, both domestic and wild, made a lot of noise. The wild parrots were hilarious to watch but also vicious and destructive, depending on the breed. She learned to trust the dogs and watch their reactions to things. The sheep had a healthy respect for the dogs and obeyed them instantly, but she didn't hold the flock too closely as they grazed over the pasture. Sitting at night by her fire while smoking her pipe, Mel realized how happy she truly was. She was completely alone except for the dogs, and she loved it. She realized that the nights spent around the fire back when she was herding cattle had only been a small taste of this. This was what she wanted. She wanted to learn as much as she could about sheep and eagerly looked forward to lambing.

She realized her mistake when Foster put another man on her flock a week later, bringing her in so she could learn about lambing. The first of the lambs had dropped, and he taught her how to tell the difference between a ewe merely giving birth and a ewe mewling in distress.

"Put your hand in there," he said, grinning as she gingerly put her hand into the birth canal and found her hand being squeezed painfully by the contractions. It was a fascinating but disgusting process, and she worked with her fingers trying to figure out the placement of the limbs inside. Usually, problems arose when a ewe was having two, three, or even four lambs. They would get stuck or wrapped up in each other, making it difficult for the ewe to give birth. Pushing limbs back and trying to figure out which one should come out first was a puzzle she enjoyed, but she really felt for the poor ewes. They seemed so vulnerable, and they never fought back, simply accepting their fates complacently as they strained to birth their offspring. They accepted most of their offspring with a bit of surprise when she had managed to draw them out with the ewe's help. Occasionally, one big lamb got stuck, but this was rare. The mothers never bleated, knowing they had to stay quiet for the sake of their young.

"Gonna have to cut that one out," Foster told her when he had checked it out with his own hand and found that the lamb was bloated. "If she survives, she likely won't be able to breed again. Damn, I hate losing a prime ewe to things like this." He notched her ear with his knife, so they knew she was game to be butchered at any time.

Sometimes, ewes rejected their lambs, but it was usually a second or a third lamb that she didn't have enough milk for. Foster showed Mel how to fool other ewes into taking these lambs, using a dead lamb's skin, which he cut and put over the new lamb. The ewe would sniff it suspiciously, making sure it was *her* lamb, before licking it and allowing it to nurse.

"If'n you get them to nurse, that's half the battle," he explained. He was, however, a little more accepting of the losses once he took the time to try and trick the ewes. Losses were expected, and there were too many sheep to take the time to coddle a lamb if it didn't thrive right away. Mel had a lot of thoughts on this but kept them to herself. She knew her soft heart bled with every lamb that was put on the burning pile, but there were too many of the living to dwell on it as she went on to other ewes that needed her help. At night when she was trying to sleep if exhaustion didn't take her right away, she thought of ways to save more of the lambs.

Enough ewes gave birth without help that the odds were in the favor of the grazer. Still, it was a precarious time for all the work involved in raising sheep.

Exhaustion became Mel's companion, and Foster worked her and the other men hard as the lambing continued for weeks. Attracted by the smell of afterbirth and the vulnerable lambs, predators came. Even in a well-populated area there were wild dogs called dingoes that the men shot with impunity.

"It's worse out in the Outback where they don't fear man," one of the men stated.

Mel, always eager to hear more about the Outback, listened unashamedly.

The man told of his time out there, shuddering as he told how lonely it was and how the nights felt oppressive. "If I had seen a bunyip, I'd have been gone sooner," he told them, and the others chuckled.

"What's a bunyip?" Mel asked, her American accent never more apparent.

They explained it was an aboriginal monster of sorts that preyed on the unsuspecting. Usually found near water, it pulled men and animals into the night, and no trace was ever found of them.

"It's got piercing eyes, but that's all anyone ever says as that's all they've seen, if they've see them at all," the man contributed, laughing, so Mel didn't know if this were a real creature here in Australia or something he had made up.

After all the sheep had given birth, they began the mulesing— removing the lamb's tails—and removing strips of wool-bearing skin from around their anus at the same time. This was to prevent their feces and urine from clotting in the wool, which could give a place for flies to lay their eggs and cause parasitic infection. At the same time, they took the opportunity to castrate most of the male lambs. Instead of using a sharp knife as they had with the mulesing, some of the men used their teeth to rip the miniscule balls from the lamb, their mouths bloody as they smiled and spit out the tiny bits of flesh. Mel tried not to get sick over the display, laughing with the others as they companionably cut the lambs, then nicked their ears to indicate they were wethers.

Over the months spent on the selection, she learned a lot and felt better for it. Foster paid her for her work and waved her on her way as she returned to Sydney to consider what she wanted to do now. She knew she would like to become a grazer. She had reached that decision on the long nights around her lonely campfire while watching the sheep. She knew she could get a license to become a grazer for only a few guineas. While riding her horse, she decided she would do that tomorrow. She wanted to take a flock into the Outback. There was land for the taking there and no one had any claim to it. She'd be alone, and that suited her fine.

She checked into a hotel and changed into her citified clothes, finding she now preferred the outfits worn by the men who grazed sheep: a stockman's hat, a simple button-up shirt, and the miner's pants. It was comfortable, unpresuming, and suited her. Wearing one of her suits, she went to dinner, listening abstractedly to conversation around her as for the first time in a long time, she ate a meal she hadn't cooked herself around the fire or the cook hadn't prepared for her and the men.

As she was listening to the conversations around her, she overheard a distinctly American accent. It had a hint of Latina or Californios

Hispanic, but it was distinct in that it was American. Her head swiveled as she looked around the dining room.

CHAPTER FOUR

"We'll have to find this lawyer and see about taking a wagon and supplies out to the station," the woman was saying to one of her men.

Mel saw that the men were vaqueros, Spanish cowboys, and she saw that the waiter didn't appreciate waiting on these dark-skinned men. She smiled to see the distinctive outfits they were wearing. There were typically western but with a flare that was unique. She listened unashamedly to their conversation.

"Do you think we should bring stock to the station?" one of the men was asking her.

"Perhaps. I don't know how many sheep they have out there, but I want to be sure to contribute."

"Your horses should be enough of a contribution," one of the older men was saying, his dark moustache tinged with a bit of gray.

"I can't believe the brazen attempts to take them away," she said, lowering her voice, so Mel had to strain to hear her. "It was a good idea to leave some of the men to guard my babies."

Babies? Mel was confused until she realized that the woman was talking about horses. Babies, indeed!

Finally, Mel was done with her excellent meal and could no longer sit there without being obvious. She knew a couple of the men had looked around and caught her listening because their voices had lowered, and the others had followed suit. They'd switched to Spanish, but having learned Castilian Spanish, Mel followed along, although some of the words required a little thought. She got up after paying for her meal and headed for their rather large table.

"Ma'am," she said, taking off the stockman's hat she had just put back on. "I couldn't help but overhear your accent. You are from California?"

Carmen looked up and saw the tall man, who whipped off his hat politely. He too had an American accent, and she smiled politely. "Yes, we are," she said in a tone that was inquiring.

"I am Mel Lawrence," she told her politely. "I'm originally from the east coast, but I have been through your beautiful state. I couldn't help but overhear you are going out to a station?" she asked, including the glowering vaqueros as she looked around. She knew that a strange man didn't usually approach a Hispanic woman, and this woman was particularly well-guarded.

"I am Carmen Pearson," the woman said, her slight accent sounding beautiful to Mel and further enhancing the natural good looks of this woman. She put out a hand that Mel captured, originally intending to shake it, then on impulse, she lifted the hand to kiss the back as she had

seen other men do. She grinned unrepentedly when she saw the men bristle.

Carmen was amused. It was so gallant and so old-fashioned. She saw her men didn't like the strange man but felt that was on principle since their job was to protect her. Many of them were distant cousins of her mother's and felt it was their duty. "What brings you to Australia, Mr. Lawrence?" she asked, her eyes twinkling.

"I was shanghaied outside San Francisco," she admitted. "It's a long story, but I've decided to stay. I too am heading inland. When I heard an accent from back home, I couldn't stop myself from making your acquaintance."

"That's very kind of you, Mr. Lawrence. I would love to hear your story?" she answered, intrigued by the large man. There was something here that she couldn't quite put her finger on, but perhaps it was just that the man was a stranger. She waved to indicate a vacant chair.

"I would love to speak with you, but I must seek my bed. It has been a long day for me, and I have business to attend to in the morning. Will you be staying in Sydney long?"

"Only a few days, just long enough to rest. I brought a herd of horses, and they must get settled after that long boat ride before we set off to our station. Perhaps we will see each other again, and you can tell me more of your story then?"

"I would like that, Miss Pearson."

"Oh, it's Mrs. Pearson," she corrected automatically.

Mel had already noticed that there was no ring on her finger but accepted her word. She nodded. "Good night, Mrs. Pearson." She smiled towards the still glowering men, nodding as well as she included them in her farewell before bowing slightly towards the woman and excusing herself.

"That was forward," Paco hissed before he could help himself, his moustache bristling angrily.

Carmen cocked an eyebrow towards her Segundo, or second, who squirmed almost immediately. Since they had left the Americas, he had felt very protective towards his employer. It was a self-inflicted duty, but he felt fatherly towards her. They were distantly related, as were almost all her men, so it meant they were all loyal to her. "Paco do not presume to direct my behavior. He was polite and interesting, and perhaps he can give us information from his own observations in this foreign land."

He blushed as he nodded, accepting her criticism as his due. They finished their meal, all feeling that the food could have used some more spices.

Mel found out where she could get a grazer license and paid her few guineas before heading back to the hotel to change into her woman's garb. It felt odd to wear these clothes after so many months wearing men's clothing, but she had to go to the bank and see if her funds had finally arrived, and she couldn't go as Mel Lawrence, the man. She found she *much* preferred wearing men's clothing, even the suits she'd had made.

"Yes, Miss Lawrence. Everything is in order as you requested, and a check has even been delivered by the Wellington Firm," the bank manager told her, treating her much better than he had before her funds had been transferred. Mel wondered how well he would treat her if he knew this was only a portion of the many funds she had available to her.

"Yes, that was an investment I made while I waited for this," her hands indicated the paperwork from her New York bank. "I'll be using some of the funds for additional investments here in Sydney as well as for my travel."

"Oh, you are vacationing around our country?" he asked, sounding condescending.

"Perhaps," she answered noncommittally, not willing to tell him of her plans as she felt it was none of his business. "I want to be sure I understand how to write out a withdrawal form for the funds in my account in your bank?" She knew she sounded flighty, as a woman should to men such as this, but she also wanted access to her funds at any amount as she saw fit. "I also wish to add another co-signer to my account?" Mel knew that she would accidentally sign 'Mel Lawrence' and in some cases it would be difficult to explain 'Melissa,' so she took the opportunity to fix that now. Let them think it was her non-existent brother or cousin.

He showed her how to complete the withdrawal form, taking that opportunity to touch her shoulder. Mel flinched but then realized it wasn't her he was interested in, just the amount in her bank account. She wasn't used to being touched, and she found it repellent that this man would try to use sex as an inducement. She supposed some women wouldn't know any better, but she did. She got out of there as soon as she could, angry at the inappropriate touch. She supposed if she had been responsive to his touch, he would have taken that as encouragement, and a dinner invitation would have followed as he courted her for her bank account. That thought angered her further, but she had other things to do and headed determinedly for the dress shop.

"Miss Lawrence!" the seamstress said, pleased to see her after so many months. She'd used the simpler designs Mel had requested on several day dresses for other customers, who had been just as pleased as Mel with the result.

"Mrs. Waters," she answered, just as pleased to see her.

"Do you need another dress or two?"

"No, I'm here on other business, if you have a moment?"

"Of course," she answered, glancing at the two seamstresses busy in the back room as she stepped forward into the storefront for some privacy.

"I noticed how busy you were when I was last here, and I wondered if you could use an investor."

"An investor?" she asked, her forehead puckering as she frowned.

"Yes, an investor that would give you money to expand your store...perhaps also a bigger and better location, more seamstresses, and a sewing machine?" Mel noticed how dreamy the woman looked immediately at hearing the words sewing machine. She'd seen some of the early models back in America, and they didn't look hard to use. She herself had sewn often enough that she knew it would be a time saver.

"You know of someone who would invest?"

"Yes...me."

"You?" She seemed confused.

"Yes, me. Think about it, madam. A man wouldn't invest in a woman's dress shop. You could expand almost immediately." She gestured to the back of the crowded store where dresses in various stages of completion were stacked. The front was kept clear for clients, but really, there was nowhere for them to go. "You could have a dressing room for your clientele, maybe even bigger windows to display your wares?" she gestured to the front, and the woman looked with her as she envisioned it. "Perhaps, you could have some of your bolts of cloth on display for the potential dress customers?"

"And how much would you invest?" the woman asked, suddenly all business.

"How much would you need?" Mel countered as they discussed it, determining how much she would need and agreeing on a satisfactory amount.

"How much would you ask as a return on this investment?" she asked later after they had dreamed over the expansion.

"Forty percent," Mel said blandly to see if the woman would bite.

Mrs. Waters gasped. "Twenty," she countered.

"Thirty, and we will have an outside firm do the books."

"You don't trust me?" she asked, suddenly sounding outraged.

"It isn't that I don't trust you, Mrs. Waters. I must trust you, or I wouldn't be here offering to invest in your business. I just thought that freeing you up from the daily accounting activities would be better for your creative soul," she said, appealing to the woman's vanity.

Mrs. Waters considered for a moment. The conversation had already excited her with all the ideas, plans, and opportunities. Suddenly, she stuck her hand out as she had seen men do. "Done!" she said, hoping everything would work out.

Mel smiled, wondering if her banker could recommend a solicitor to draw up the papers of their partnership as she was shaking Mrs. Waters' hand. "Done." They continued to discuss their plans including how much Mel would invest in total and where the new shop would be located. Mrs. Waters felt it should be on the same street but in a larger store, so people could easily find her.

"There is that store on the corner that has been available for a while, but I bet the rent is outrageous," Mrs. Waters pointed down the street.

Mel considered, nodding. "I'll have my solicitor draw up the paperwork, and he will come with the check after you have signed. Please hire your own solicitor to review the contract, so you are comfortable with our deal."

Mrs. Waters agreed as her mind whirled with plans. She had thought it would take years to expand her little store. She'd often had to turn away people who wanted dresses made and wondered if that had been wise. Still, other customers had been forced to wait longer than she would have liked. A sewing machine! How fancy. She could send out notices to her current clients announcing the new store when it was ready. She could also have cards made with the name of her establishment and its new location printed on them, naming herself as the proprietor. She was very excited with all her plans as Mel left.

Mel returned to the bank to ask for the name of a reputable solicitor. She was surprised to get an appointment that same day. The bank manager's name opened doors, and she remembered that for the future. It wasn't much different in the States; it was always who you knew. Not only would the solicitor draw up the papers for her business with Mrs. Waters, but he knew the owner of the vacant shop that the dressmaker had mentioned as a possible new location.

"It would be a better investment to buy that building and rent it out to the dress shop. Being on a corner, it would get a lot of interest because both sets of windows are visible to the casual shopper. The upstairs has two apartments to rent out as well. I know they are occupied now, but one of the renters is leaving, and perhaps, the dressmaker might want to live in one? Maybe even one or two of her seamstresses is looking for a place to rent?"

Mel was pleased because the solicitor didn't treat her as a *mere* woman. He genuinely wanted her to succeed. He suggested an accounting firm that would keep track of the books for them, and in a few days, Mel was the owner of the store that Mrs. Waters had pointed out. Within weeks, the dressmaker could move into the shop, rent out the upstairs to her own employees as an incentive, and hire more people. She had already ordered the sewing machine once the paperwork had been signed and the check delivered. Mrs. Waters was surprised to find out Mel was her landlord, but she had been generous in her terms to the dress shop and the new location had more than doubled her space. Mrs. Waters immediately felt the difference in her clientele and knew the rent was worth it.

Mel hadn't been idle. She'd changed back into her stockman clothes and had gone down to the stockyard in order to inquire about purchasing dogs, sheep, and horses for the station she intended to establish in the Outback. Sheep born in the Australian spring and American fall were already mulesed and castrated, a process she hadn't enjoyed learning as she remembered having to watch while some men used their teeth instead of cutting with the knife, her preferred technique. She had learned that once the sheep were sheared, the price immediately fell off, and she was waiting to find a large flock.

"I've got four dogs I'll let ya have for a price," one man told her as he found her inquiring about the animals. "They're proven," he confided, which meant they would herd and weren't untried. Dogs that were raised to herd sheep and showed no interest in herding were frequently bashed over the head or put down immediately as they were of no use to a grazer.

Mel wanted a dozen dogs, knowing she might lose some on the trip and worrying about how large a flock she could handle on her own. She also wanted some dogs that she could breed since this would be a growing operation in time. In the meantime, she had acquired a wagon, storing it at the stockyards as she filled it with supplies.

"Buying up Australia?" Carmen teased when they met in the stockyard, of all places.

"Mrs. Pearson. It's always a delight to see you," Mel returned as she turned from the animals she was perusing. The sheep looked terrible with their long, wooly coats shorn. Some still had splotches of wool on them, and others had nicks and cuts from the shears. She lifted her hat respectfully but didn't remove it in the hot Australian sun.

"Do you know where you are going in the Outback?"

"Not sure yet. Thought I'd go to the end of the tracks and on into the never-never," she admitted, the thought not so far from her actual plans.

"We are going out to a station I own with my distant cousins. Why don't we travel together?"

"Your men wouldn't like that," she pointed out, glancing towards two of them that were far enough away to give the woman privacy but close enough to guard her in the event a man approached her.

"No, they wouldn't; however, that doesn't dictate what I do, and we do have to get going. I've spent enough time here in Sydney. I was hoping to buy some sheep too," she indicated the poor animals in one of the corrals near where they were standing.

"Slim pickings," Mel mentioned, and then a commotion near the front of the stockyards drew both their attention. Her dogs, sitting around her feet and panting, perked up at the mass of sheep that men were even now herding into several corrals.

"What's going on?" Carmen murmured as they both started walking towards the uproar.

"I have no idea," Mel stated as she signaled to the four dogs and they followed at heel instantly. She hadn't made them work since she bought them, but they did guard her wagon for her after she fed them and left them to return to her hotel nightly.

The dust the sheep kicked up was intense, and both women used handkerchiefs to cover their mouths and noses. Carmen's handkerchief was a delicate Queen Anne piece of lace and Mel's was a red bandana that reminded her of American, which she had found in a store.

"What's going on?" Mel asked one of the men as he closed a paddock that was packed full of the sheep.

"Bank confiscation," he said with a grin, glancing at Carmen more than once and hoping to catch her eye.

"What does that mean?" Mel asked for them both, suddenly feeling protective of Carmen and glancing around, not surprised to see Paco and one of the other men a few paces off.

"Some bloke ordered these from England, but he ran outta money before they arrived, and the bank confiscated 'em."

Mel looked at the sheep. They were Merinos, the very breed that Foster had told her was one of the best for wool production. The others in the other paddocks paled by comparison. These also had full coats and hadn't been sheared yet, judging by the lengths of wool on their bodies. "How many are there?" she asked, speculating as she eyed them.

"Over five thousand," he bragged, still trying to catch Carmen's eye but failing. Still, he answered Mel as though she were talking for the Hispanic beauty.

"Who do I talk to about buying 'em?" she asked.

"Yank, yer gonna have to wait for the auction just like everyone else," he said as he turned to hurry and help with the other sheep being put in another paddock, filling the small space end to end with the hapless animals.

"I'll go halves," Carmen murmured when she saw Mel's determined look.

Mel turned to look down on the petite woman in surprise. She had almost forgotten Carmen was there as she thought about what obtaining the sheep would mean.

Just then, more sheep arrived, followed by another group of men with even more sheep. She had never seen the stockyards this full, but it explained why they had so many pens that often sat empty. They could easily accommodate thousands of animals. She looked down at her dogs. They were shaking with excitement at the idea of helping, and she could tell they were barely constraining themselves, only obeying her because she had fed them, and their loyalty was now to her.

"Let's see what else we can find out," she advised as she nodded. She wanted all five thousand for herself but didn't know if she could handle that many. She wasn't prepared yet to hire additional shepherds to work for her, or as the Australians called them, stockmen. She didn't even know where she was going.

It was Paco who found out there were eight thousand sheep, and he also learned which bank owned them. Mel and Carmen headed for the bank to ask about purchasing them outright and not waiting for the auction. Mel had a good idea how much they were worth unshorn, and she discussed it with the woman as they rode towards the bank. The two men followed them, guarding the senora, and looking menacingly at anyone who even looked sideways at the woman. The four dogs followed Mel's horses' hooves, keeping an eye out, so they didn't get trampled. Mel figured they could use the exercise and besides, it was a way to keep their focus off the temptation of the sheep.

"They are to go up for auction," the bank manager stated loftily.

"Mr. Allen, I'm sure that I could make this easier for you," Mel stated. "Your bank stands to lose money on the deal since the owner forfeited them."

"How did you–?" he began, but Mel interrupted. She lifted a hand to silence the man, something a woman wouldn't have dared to do and would never have been allowed to get away with. He glanced from the large *man* to the petite woman next to Mel.

"I'm sure you understand how these rumors get started. The animals have just come from a long voyage and are in poor shape. You are going to have to shear them, if they survive, and that will reduce their value by half." She saw him start at the phrase, *'if they survive.'*

"We are willing to pay you for them outright," she dangled the offer, "and that will save you the cost of having them sheared."

"I don't even know you…" he began, his suspicions raised by the Yank's accent as well as the dusky beauty who accompanied him and hadn't said anything.

"You can check with the Bank of England. My account will be used for this transaction, and they will assure you I have the funds," she said firmly, using the snobby tone she had acquired defensively back in her New York days.

"And you are?"

"Mel Lawrence," she returned, not even considering using her full name with Carmen Pearson listening.

He had heard the name. Bankers were a tight group and congregated often, and the story of a Yank transferring those kinds of funds to the Bank of England branch here in Sydney had been titillating gossip. The name didn't sound quite right, but it had been a while since he had heard it discussed, and he could be remembering wrong. "Would you be willing to pay what they are worth in England?"

"Come now, man. They have just gotten off a ship from England, they barely survived the crossing, and they look terrible." Mel wasn't going to admit they had looked quite good, considering the trip. It was obvious the animals had been well taken care of on the journey. "If I take them–" she began but Carmen interrupted.

"If *we*…" she breathed, clutching slightly at Mel's elbow to remind her she was there.

Mel looked down and saw the twinkle in the woman's eye. Carmen knew she was bargaining with the banker and not fooled at all. The banker, however, didn't know stock. By the time they agreed to buy

the entire flock as is, they had wheedled the price down considerably, but it was a cash deal, and the banker was pleased to have gotten anything for the poor, diseased, and apparently dying sheep. He accepted a bank draft from both Americans, each paying for half the deal, and he signed the animals over to them.

"Now, what?" Carmen asked with a grin as they left the bank, the bill of sale made out to them both.

"I guess we get our sheep sheared and finish stocking up for the trip out to your station. I'll see what I can find nearby when we split up the flock."

"Maybe you will be one of my neighbors," Carmen said generously, having no idea what she would find when she got out to Twin Station where her cousins were running the sheep station. They were her reluctant partners, and she wondered how they would feel about her purchase. The lawyer here in Sydney had tried to get her to sell out several times since she had arrived. She'd perversely stayed in the large city to get the lay of the land, but it was time she headed out. Her men would be pleased as they were restless.

"Maybe," Mel agreed, delighted with her purchase as they headed back to the stockyards. She felt the deal was an absolute bargain.

When the auction was cancelled, they disappointed quite a few people, who had looked forward to buying some of the sheep and were hoping to get a bargain themselves. Finding out that the auction was off, and the two Yanks had bought the entire flock, created some ill will. Mel watched as the sheep were sheared, learning how to do it herself. She was disappointed to note that some of the anger towards her and Carmen for purchasing the sheep out from under the noses of the more experienced grazers continued. The shearers swore at the animals, nicked them, and generally treated their sheep badly.

"Easy there. Either cut him evenly or get another job," she warned one of the shearers menacingly when she saw the slipshod job he was doing.

"Yeah? Whatcha going to do about it?" he challenged, getting up from where he had been bending over the sheep while shearing it.

Mel didn't hesitate, knowing that waiting and posturing was pointless. She also knew if they discovered she was a woman; it wouldn't go well with her. She hit the man with one hard right to his unprotected jaw, and he went down. He almost appeared to be flying as he also tripped over the downed sheep he had been shearing. He was out cold. Mel looked around for other troublemakers, but the other shearers resumed work on their own animals, clipping a little more carefully as they took off the sheep's long, wool coats.

"I don't think we'll have any more problems with them," Carmen commented after she had observed her partner taking down the man. She hadn't followed through with the man, and one of his mates had picked the stunned man up off the floor when he began to come around. He had gone back to work and was doing a more careful job now.

The men got paid by the number of sheep they clipped, no matter how long the wool, and eight thousand sheep were quickly defrocked. The wool was taken away to be shipped to mills in England.

Mel and Carmen both filled wagons with supplies of peas, rice, salt pork, flour, and other necessities that were frequently shipped inland to the various stations. Mel met the rest of the dozen men traveling with Carmen as they readied for the long trip. Some had families of their own, and she liked quite a few of them. Carmen's children were a

hoot, but their nursemaids seemingly disapproved of the Yank they had heard so much about from the men. A guide, who had been to Twin Station and was taking their annual supplies to them, agreed to travel with them and show them the way. Four wagons left the stockyards to meet up with the drayage company's wagons, including Mel's, which Carmen had bought from her. Mel had purchased two more dogs, and Carmen had found five, so eleven dogs worked around the flock as they set out. Yet another was acquired by Paco as they drove the large flock west along Paramatta Road in a long line.

"You sure about this trip?" Carmen asked as she admired the large Brumby horse that Mel had acquired. The two other packhorses she had bought were also of this wild, sturdy, but shaggy breed. Mel was admiring the two dozen horses Carmen had shipped from America, wishing she could afford them, but the woman wasn't selling anyway, which was attested by the many offers she had received and declined for the fine beasts. Still, Mel had put in for one of their offspring when they became available, knowing her new friend would hold it for her even if it was years in the making.

"Nope, I'm not sure about this trip, but I'm willing to go wherever my heart is sending me," she replied cryptically.

Carmen had figured out Mel's secret after their first week on the trip, but she understood the large woman's need to keep it and didn't pry. She respected her too much to reveal her secret. She let on that she knew, but from the little she had gleaned about her being shanghaied and ostracized by her peers back in New England, she thought she understood why the woman would rather go about as a man. She certainly had more freedom as a man; the transaction at the bank had proven that. She also sensed Mel's attraction to her, and while it pleased her vanity, the feeling wasn't returned.

Mel had been pleased to meet Carmen's children. Their maturity was a surprise as they rode along on horses belonging to their mother, not the least bit intimidated by their size, and showing no fear of Dancer, the stallion that Carmen rode. She didn't ride sidesaddle, and they were well supplied with western saddles, one of which Mel purchased. She didn't like that the Australian saddles had no pommels, and she felt more comfortable in the familiar Western saddle.

They continued west on the track toward what they were assured would take them to Menindee. They had to cross a river there that was described as 'so muddy that the good water was buried under all the silt.' Some said it ran upside down, and Carmen had appreciated the humor of that. Used to the clean waters coming out of the Sierra Nevada Mountains in California, she missed the cold, clear water. She'd enjoyed the Blue Mountains here in New South Wales as they traveled through them but was told that wasn't even a quarter of the trip on their way to Twin Station where they were headed.

She had a lot to think about on this trip, like meeting Mel Lawrence, the American who had assured her he had been shanghaied. Mel had confided in her but only after Carmen had accidentally discovered his secret. Mel Lawrence was not a big boned, burly man, but a big boned, burly woman. Melissa Lawrence had mistakenly been taken for a man because of her short hair and mannish attire as well her size. Not willing to be gang-raped on the vessel that had absconded with her person, she let them think she was a man, hiding her sexuality from them in the months it had taken to cross the vast ocean from San Francisco. Because she worked so hard, they didn't suspect the large

person was a woman and simply accepted her at face value as a man. Carmen realized now that the two vessels, Mel's and her own transporting her worldly goods, horses, and people, had left many months apart.

Mel had also asked that Carmen keep her secret, which she willingly agreed to. She knew there was probably a good reason for the secrecy and hoped to someday find out what it was. The two Americans had become good friends in this foreign land, and both were heading for the Outback.

CHAPTER FIVE

As they were coming out of the Blue Mountains, heading for Bathurst and then past it onto the rolling hills, they encountered drays pulled by bullocks and oxen that were bringing back mounds of wool from the various stations. This group of men were a cordial lot, anxious to get back to Sydney, and one of them owned an aboriginal woman. The Americans camped near them and listened to the boisterous talk and bragging of a few of the men, some seemingly intent on impressing the Yanks. Some even tried to flirt with the senora, not in the least intimidated by the vaqueros she had traveling with her. When the big Yank backed up the senora, there were a few that backed down. They didn't realize that the Hispanic men protecting Carmen were far more of a threat.

The men were interested in the large flock of sheep the Americans were taking into the Outback and exchanged information. Mel was watching how the carter treated the aboriginal woman and decided to challenge the men to a game of cards. She played to their vanities and finally enticed the one named Bradley, who apparently owned the woman, to play cards. She didn't even have to use the tricks she had learned so long ago in New Orleans to win against the man. His confidence, ego, and overweening pride kept him in the game. Mel let him think he was a good player, keeping him in the game until he borrowed against the woman's value, and then, she let him lose. Mel had to get a little forceful to collect her bet, but the man eventually sulkily paid his bet and turned the woman over to the big Yank.

"What are you going to do with her?" Carmen asked Mel, referring to the chained, Australian Aborigine she had acquired.

"Free her," Mel said shortly and succinctly. It had never occurred to her to keep the woman. She looked at the collar and attached chain around the woman's neck as well as the chains around the woman's ankles distastefully.

Carmen nodded, never doubting her friend or her decision to acquire the woman. The woman looked afraid, ready to bolt, but Mel tried to lessen her fear by communicating with her.

"Dog...daaawg," she said, drawing the word out and pointing at the dogs as they came in to eat that first night.

Alinta tried to repeat the word. She realized her new man expected her to learn his language, but some sounds were difficult for her, no matter how hard she tried. Still, she was eager to learn, and she realized that communicating with these white men would be a good thing. She was surprised they were heading back towards the Outback with the wagons...way-guns the man called them. She wondered if she could get back to her family. Then, she realized her family would never accept her back. Her father had abandoned her once her value was gone. Realizing her family was forever gone to her, she decided to make the best of what was before her. The man was kindly to her and was teaching her his white words. She looked about more now, not always staring down and trying to avoid being noticed by the men. She was no longer being used, and Mel had supplied her with more clothing.

They stopped in the next town where Mel sought out a blacksmith to remove the collar and chain, selling the metal back to the man. Mel looked on curiously as the blacksmith removed the restraints, never having seen a slave collar before. She was alarmed to see the only way to remove it was by sheer force.

Alinta struggled at first. She hadn't understood the collar when it was first put on, and now, she was not willing to have another attached. Mel held her firmly as the man removed it, the wool between the metal and her neck falling away. Alinta felt wonderingly at her neck when Mel put her back on her feet and smiled at her. The collar, despite the wool padding, had chafed, and Alinta immediately felt the loss of the weight from the heavy iron. She looked at the despised collar as Mel

offered it up to the other man, who negotiated for the used iron. It was a commodity he could use in his blacksmith shop.

Next, Mel headed for a store. They frowned when the aboriginal woman came inside but shut their mouths as Mel quickly looked for ready-made clothing and paid for it with cash. Her size alone kept them from ordering the Aborigine out of their store. Alinta didn't understand at first when Mel held up clothes to her body to see if they would fit. First, she held up shirts and then, miner's pants and underwear. A small, almost childlike stockman's hat completed the outfit, and Alinta carried it all, not understanding it was for her to keep. As Mel headed back to their camp outside the small town, Alinta followed, hurrying to keep up with the taller man's long strides.

Mel allowed Alinta other freedoms. Her gathering stick had been lost when she was captured, and Alinta searched among the deadfalls for another that she could fashion, using stones to smooth it. Mel watched, wishing she could ask the aboriginal woman about what she was doing. Still, the word game, as she termed it, was coming along, and Alinta had a phenomenal memory. Carmen and her children enjoyed playing along as they helped the woman learn. She remembered all the words she had acquired, only having to repeat them two or three times before they were hers. Mel was surprised that the woman appeared to have no words for dog or horse in her own language. The closest she came to dog was dingo, and that seemed universal. The wild dogs were usually heard at night as they trailed their large flock for a time, but the combined smell of man and dogs seemed to be a deterrent. However, as they traveled and entered other territories, new packs of the wild dogs tried their patience as they attempted to make a meal of their sheep.

Alinta took an interest in their cooking too, amazed at the bounty that was in their wagons. The rice and peas were a favorite of hers, but she didn't really like the fat from the mutton, preferring the meat to be nearly raw. Salt pork was a taste that left her in awe, and beef was her favorite meat. She searched for and found seeds and other things off the trail as Mel allowed her to roam, only worrying once or twice that she had run off.

"She'll have to go eventually, won't she?" Carmen asked as they rode their horses at the front of the column. The dust that the sheep kicked up on the track made it impossible for them to ride the drag too often.

"I hope she will be happy to be returned to her family," Mel said, watching the Aborigine effortlessly club a lizard and put it into the bag she had given her. Alinta had been amazed at the bag, which was much finer than any she could have woven from the Australian grass called spinifex. She had turned it over and over after Mel gave it to her, examining it closely.

"You think they will want her back?" Carmen asked knowingly.

"I have no idea. That's one thing I hope to ask her as she learns English." Mel did worry. The woman, almost a girl, seemed cheerful, well-meaning, and bright. Did she want to go back to her family? There were many things she wanted to ask her, but the language barrier was only part of the problem. The woman didn't seem to have what Mel would have termed common sense. She didn't seem to understand that things could be broken, that not everything was made from iron. Mel had cringed when Alinta accidentally broke a bottle and their cook, one of Carmen's men, had started yelling in consternation over the broken glass. The Spanish phrases sounded musical, but the cook's tone had frightened the wild woman.

"Easy there, easy. It can be replaced, right, Jose?" Mel asked as she came running up where Alinta cowered, expecting a blow to fall. She pulled the girl up and into her arms. She towered over her at least a foot, and her heart went out to the terrified girl.

"Si, si," he said contritely, having sworn and become upset over the mess of glass in his carefully prepared food. He began shoveling the food into the fire. No one could eat food that had glass in it. "I am sorry, Alinta," he said, trying to touch her on the arm, but she cringed away. His face told her how sorry he was as he watched her.

Alinta may not understand the words, but tone told a lot more, and his body language gave away a lot more than he intended. She looked at him wonderingly, trying to understand him, and little clues gave her ideas about what was being said. She realized that Mel was holding her, but not so hard that she couldn't get away if she wanted. She looked up at the big man in as much wonder as she had looked at Jose. Realizing no one was angry at her, and no one was going to strike her, she relaxed. She heard the concern in Mel's voice towards the man, his name seemed to be Jose, and she began to fit these things together in her mind. Things had changed a lot for this primitive woman, and she was trying to figure out these white people.

Alinta could see that Mel and Carmen were vastly different white people, and although the Hispanic people were dark too and getting darker from the hot, Australian sun, they were still a lot lighter than her own people. She didn't think of them as Hispanic because that hadn't been explained to her, but at the same time, she wouldn't have understood yet. Mel was obviously one of those white men, but

nothing like the ones who had captured her. Her kindness alone intrigued the aboriginal woman.

"Did Alinta do something bad?" Rachel, Carmen's young daughter, asked worriedly as she came running up.

"No, it was an accident," Mel explained to the little girl, her voice softening.

Alinta was fascinated by Carmen's children, not having seen white children this close before. The ones she had seen in the towns they traveled through never came near the wild woman. The offering of friendship between the children, even temporarily for an evening, was immediately accepted, and she watched avidly as they played together. Remembering her own childhood long ago, she wondered at the child growing inside her. She was aware of its movement now, even if her belly showed only a slight bulge.

Alinta left the safety of Mel's arms to help Jose. He was surprised by her attempts to help him clean up, and then she cut herself on the glass, not understanding that it was sharp, and the shards were dangerous.

"She's bleeding. Alinta's bleeding!" Rachel announced, seeing the blood.

Alinta put her thumb wonderingly in her mouth. She tasted the food, the dirt, and the blood on it immediately, then spat it out.

Mel gently pulled Alinta's thumb from her mouth and handed her a handkerchief, which she showed her how to wrap around the bleeding thumb. The red color of the material seemed to fascinate the woman as she stared at it. Mel applied pressure, amused at the primitive woman's fascination and wondering what would happen to her when they parted ways. She too had noticed the rounding belly and knew it wasn't just from their good food. She felt strangely maternal towards the woman, but at the same time, she cared for her and worried what would happen when they found more aboriginal people and she went with them.

CHAPTER SIX

They traveled steadily west, and the temperatures got hotter and hotter. They tried to stop near ponds, or billabongs as they called them here in Australia, whenever they could. Creaks or streams were not plentiful, and the farther west they went, the less water there would be.

As their large flock and contingent paused at the top of a hill that led down to a large river, their guide announced it was Menindee, pointing to the track that was visible on the opposite side of the river.

"You'll have to arrange for the ferry to take your sheep across, Missus," he addressed Carmen, since she was going to the station where he was taking these supplies. He didn't trust the men who rode with her, but an attractive woman always seemed to garner not only compliments but also flirtation and respect. The big man, who frequently rode with her, the other Yank, he grudgingly respected but

only because he had heard of the one punch knockout in the shearing sheds back in Sydney. He'd eyed the man several times but knew better than to start anything with him. The big American was curious about everything and frequently asked about animals, birds, grasses, and even the trees they encountered. His men kept well away from the big man for the most part, just in case they unintentionally offended him.

Mel didn't differentiate between the men hauling supplies to Twin Station and the vaqueros traveling with Carmen. To her, they were all just men. She found time for stories and conversations with both groups of men, who kept to themselves, not socializing as the Australian and English men found the Hispanic Californios very different. Even Mel, who they continued to call a Yank, could see similarities, but they eyed the swarthy men from the southwest part of the United States suspiciously.

Mel was grateful that the vaqueros were willing to help with the sheep. They weren't stock snobs like she had seen in the west where some men wouldn't associate with sheep ranchers and vice versa. She'd known it to come to violence, but here it seemed to be reversed. Sheep were much more numerous than cattle, and while she hoped to obtain some beef, right now, her focus was on the sheep she had purchased with Carmen.

"We'll do that," Carmen said, giving the blushing man a smile as she nodded in agreement.

"Can't we swim them across?" Mel asked, eyeing the dirty river and trying to gauge its depth. They'd swum the flock across many nameless creeks on the trek out here.

"No, sir. It's deeper than it looks," the man explained respectfully, trying to suppress his blush from being around Carmen and talk knowledgeably. He would ferry his wagons across too.

They stopped in the town to pick up a few odds and ends, and Mel arranged to load the sheep on the ferry in batches, so they could take them across the large river. Leaving some of the dogs on the other side with a couple of the men, the ferry returned to take more and more of the sheep before taking the wagons and people across.

"Someday, they will have steel rails to towns such as this," Mel commented, looking back as the town receded across the river.

"I hope it doesn't ruin the land," Carmen agreed as she imagined it.

They rode on along the track, stopping every third day or so, so the sheep could graze and maintain their weight.

"This country is larger than I had given it credit for. No wonder letters to my cousins and uncle took forever to be answered," Carmen confided as they rode along.

"Mama, do you think I could ride today?" one of the boys called from the back of the wagon where he rode with his brothers, sister, and nursemaid. The nursemaid looked exhausted from taking care of the four children.

"Don't you think it's too hot?" Carmen answered, looking at the sweat that dripped down the boy's face. She herself felt the same way and frequently used her delicate handkerchief to wipe the dust and sweat from her face. It was no longer a pristine, white lace, and she was glad she had stopped wearing her dresses and now wore the stockman's clothes that Mel had recommended she purchase back in Sydney.

"No, Mama. I think being on the back of a horse will be cooler than sitting here in the wagon. If there is any breeze, I think I will feel it better there," he insisted logically.

Carmen shared a smile with Mel. The boy would ride every day if he could. Neither of the women felt the aches in their legs anymore. They had worked those out before they had even crossed the Blue Mountains back near the coast.

"Okay, when we stop for the nooning, you can saddle one of the horses for you and your brother," she indicated the brother, who was sitting behind him looking hopeful.

"But, Mama, I wanted to ride alone," he protested, not liking the idea of sharing.

"Then, perhaps, you don't need to ride at all."

He thought about it only a second, not willing to lose the chance to ride instead of being stuck in the wagon with his younger siblings. "He can ride with me," he conceded.

"He won't last long," she assured him with a smile, and she and Mel rode on ahead of the wagon, having only stopped back by the wagons to check on Alinta, who had caught her foot on a thorn.

"Wish I could get her to wear shoes or boots," Mel groused as they checked on her, and she smiled in pleasure to see the Yank.

"Are you trying to civilize her?" Carmen questioned, amused. She remembered hearing of whites trying to civilize American Indians…and failing.

"No, not at all," Mel shook her head. "I just want her to be comfortable and safe…" she began and then left off. "Hell, she was probably comfortable wearing no clothes for generations." They'd seen a few *wild* Aborigines as they headed west, and each time, Mel

worried that Alinta would take off and go with them. So far though, she hadn't seemed to want to go with any of them even though they looked at her curiously. She was still wearing the long, white man's shirt...and that was it. The clothes that Mel had bought for her were rolled up with her bedroll and becoming all wrinkled. The hat was her one concession, and she wore it proudly.

"Thinking we can change the natives has caused more problems than anything else. My ancestors were conquistadors, and look how well that turned out," Carmen mentioned, remembering the stories of the Spanish, who came to take over Mexico, killing thousands of natives, breeding with them, and trying to conquer them. Eventually, they had civilized some, taking some as their wives, but they were far different from the original Spanish men and women their ancestors had been. Even the Californios she had known were different from those who visited from Mexico. They were becoming Americanized, and she wasn't sure that was a good thing. Still, she didn't regret leaving and was looking forward to seeing Twin Station and her inheritance.

"You've been on Twin Station for a day now," the carter told her one day as they traveled. They had been on the track for months because of the sheep slowing them down, and he could have left them behind, but because she was one of the owners, he had stayed with them. Carmen appreciated it.

"When will we be at the home paddock?" she asked, looking about the land now with a proprietorial air.

"Tomorrow," he promised, calling to one of his men to go on ahead and warn them. Carmen looked nothing like the Englishman, but she stated her uncle had been English, and he had known the man. If she had made up the whole story, why would she travel this far for nothing

with all these animals? He knew that the big Yank owned half the sheep, but he didn't know why they were traveling together.

Mel was restless that last night, wondering what they would find at Carmen's station tomorrow. Would Alinta want to leave her right away?

The carter had said there were Aborigines on the station. Maybe one of them could communicate with Alinta? Would anyone know her language? Did Mel want the woman to go? She'd enjoyed her company as Mel had taught her their ways. She showed no signs of wanting to leave, but that didn't mean she couldn't go. Mel wouldn't keep her. She wasn't into slavery, and that was essentially what that Bradley had done. The result of that was in Alinta's belly. She'd heard the woman slink off to vomit her breakfast a time or two. It didn't look like she was feeling well, and there had been many times that Mel had insisted she ride in the wagon. She would have liked to have had her up on a horse but didn't think that wise with her belly rounding. Did pregnant women ride horses? Mel had no idea. All the women of her acquaintance had basically secluded themselves away when they began to show.

The land looked arid, and as they came over the last rise, Mel rode ahead to direct the sheep away from a flock she saw grazing on the hillside. They were at least half a mile away, but if two flocks came

into the vicinity of each other, they would flow together, their herding instinct mandating it. She didn't worry about separating the flock when she left from Carmen's share, but she wanted the breed she had paid for, not the sheep she saw grazing on the stations on their way out here. Carmen had already agreed to give her three- and four-year-old sheep from the flock. These would help establish her station quicker as the animals were more likely to give birth to twins or multiple young at that age.

Two people came riding down the track as they got closer, a man and a woman, and Mel nodded to acknowledge them as she also watched the oncoming wagons and sheep. Carmen saw them too and rode up just as they reached her.

"Are you Carmen Pearson?" the man asked, eyeing Mel.

"I am Senora Carmen Valenzuela Pearson," Carmen said with a flourish of her voice as she reined up.

"Ah, cousin Carmen," the man said with a bright smile, relieved that the pretty woman was his cousin and not the other…woman? He was curious, and then, he realized it was a man…or was it? He eyed Mel and then looked back at his cousin. "I am Harold Polaski, and this is my sister, Fabiola."

At the names, Carmen's perfectly sculpted eyebrow raised.

"I know, most people don't expect such a name," Harold explained. "I believe your uncle may have had a hand in influencing the name of my sister," he said with a smile, trying to be charming.

"This is Mel Lawrence, who is traveling with us," Carmen introduced her, and Mel nodded.

Harold looked at her again, trying to figure out if she was a man or a woman. Fabiola nodded coldly, looking every inch the landowner, strong and capable. Harold looked…weak, his boyish good looks fading as he grew older. Used to being indulged a bit as he grew up, he could give the appearance of the eligible station owner but failed to keep it up for too long, as they would soon learn. "We were wondering when you would get here, but we never expected you to bring stock." He looked beyond her at the sight of the eight thousand sheep, the herd of horses, and the wagons. He looked alarmed. "We do have sheep here," he pointed out.

"Half of these are Mr. Lawrence's," Carmen explained, gesturing to Mel.

Mister. That told Harold that Mel was a man, not a woman. Fabiola looked on, not saying much as she watched the strangers.

"I also thought that having Merinos in your flock would be good for wool production," Carmen continued, almost echoing verbatim a conversation she had had with Mel many times on the trip out here. It was why they had immediately set out to obtain these sheep when they found them. Mel had repeated what she had learned of breeds, having listened to Foster and his men as well as other station owners and grazers she met.

"Then, you will be staying?" Fabiola spoke up, sounding haughty.

"Yes, I sold my ranch in California to come here. I take it you didn't get my lawyer's letters?" Carmen asked, feeling equally haughty towards the woman.

"Yes, we got your letters, but did you get our letter asking if you would be interested in us buying you out?"

"I wanted to see what I had inherited," her arm swept out towards the immense landscape around them, ignoring the question. Of course,

she had gotten the letters, dealt with the lawyers, and decided against selling.

The first of the wagons had passed by them, and the sheep were coming up. Mel moved away to help keep the sheep away from the flock that was moving away. She whistled to her dogs to keep them on the side away from the other flock. Both Harold and Fabiola watched her.

"That's a lot of Merinos," Fabiola commented, her face relaxing as she talked about the stock.

"We were lucky. They'd just come off a ship and were confiscated by the bank. Mel there recognized them for what they were, and we bought them."

"Is he your partner too?" Harold asked, puzzled, wondering at the relationship and frowning. He'd tried to remain optimistic about their distant *cousin* coming to live at the station. He had been angry that she wouldn't let them buy her out, but Fabiola had shrugged, not caring so long as they could stay on the ranch they had grown up on. There wasn't much worry about that since they owned half the station.

"No, Mr. Lawrence is planning on setting up a station, and I had hoped you two would have recommendations of where he should locate it. Perhaps a neighbor we could use?" she hinted broadly. "In the meantime, do you have the pens to accommodate this flock and my herd?"

"Of course," Harold assured her, but Fabiola watched her closely, wondering at the Hispanic woman and why she had given up a ranch in California to come here.

They rode to the top of the rise and looked down on the valley that held the home paddock. It was a large, wide valley with a creek that

meandered down the middle. The station house was situated along it as well as pens, barns, and sheds. It wasn't a large home paddock, but it was adequate, if a bit run-down. Carmen looked down on their destination and wondered at its setup, disappointed with how it looked. She hadn't expected a fine house and green pasturage after all the arid land they had driven through, but this was barren. She could see an aboriginal village on one side and what must be the station house on the other. There were large barrels on stilts for water, and the houses were also on stilts to keep out bugs and keep them above the water level of the creek when it rained.

Harold rode on ahead to get men to help with the sheep. He knew the flock was valuable with those fine Merinos and wondered how set that Lawrence person was on taking half. If he could talk him out of it, he'd be happy. Cousin Carmen was right, they would be good for increasing their wool production…if they survived. He watched as the men herded them into the paddocks, seeing how well they had traveled. It was then, he noticed the aboriginal woman and several Hispanic women with many children accompanying them. There were also a dozen men that looked swarthy to him and the usual carters, who brought their supplies. They had been long overdue, and now he understood it was because they had led his cousin out here.

For the first time since they had left Sydney, the sheep and horses were corralled, and Mel breathed a sigh of relief. They'd kept the sheep in rope corrals, or folds as they were called here, and only the sheep thought they were safe in them. The folds didn't really keep them safe, but they thought they did, and along with the dozen dogs, the patrolling men, and the guns, they managed.

Carmen was welcomed into the main house, a four-room affair with two bedrooms, a front room, and a kitchen. She looked on without saying anything, but Paco was horrified. After the large hacienda she had left in California, she should come to this…this hovel? He kept his face carefully schooled since Carmen wasn't saying anything as she looked around and learned the setup. There was no way these people could have afforded to pay her the sum they had offered her for the station based on what she was seeing.

"He can sleep in the bunkhouse with the other men, although with your other men…" Harold began hesitantly, referring to Mel.

"My vaqueros?" Carmen corrected gently, giving it the full Spanish flavor as she asked.

"Yes, your…men," he repeated himself, not even attempting to use the Spanish word, "but it's going to be a tight fit. The bunkhouse only can hold a dozen."

"What are some of those houses along the creek?" she asked.

"For some of our married stockmen…" he began slowly as he realized what she was saying. "Three of them are empty," he offered up half-heartedly. It was obvious he was reluctant to give them out, but Carmen was more than a match for him.

"Mel, you and Alinta can take one of the empty houses there along the creek," she called, seeing the large woman walking her horses along and heading for the corrals. The woman nodded and turned to what looked like an empty house.

"Paco, if the bunkhouse is full, use the other empty house for the men," she continued, taking charge. She turned back to her cousin. "There's that for now, until the drayage men return to Sydney."

"They'll go after we unload the supplies and then load the shearing," he explained.

"Yes, that's what they told me," she returned, nodding.

"They're so late," he complained but realized immediately that was the wrong thing to say.

"Yes, that's my fault since I didn't want to run down the sheep or my horses." She turned away, looking in the house and wondering where she and her children would stay.

"Senora, where should we go?" Maria asked as she came up, speaking in Spanish as was her custom.

"For now, let's just get the children settled, so they can go out and play," Carmen returned, gesturing towards the other empty house along the creek. It was obvious she was as comfortable in English as she was in Spanish.

"That's a pretty language," Harold said with a smile, trying to be charming, but it was obvious he didn't like them speaking a language he didn't understand. He watched as the other Hispanic woman began leading the children towards one of the empty houses.

Carmen ignored him, instead watching Fabiola as she got down near the sheds and started commanding the men who stood around. There was soon activity as they moved about busily. Down by the creek, an annoying noise had started. "What is that?" she asked about the noise she heard.

"Sounds like a corroboree starting," Harold said, explaining. "It's an Aborigine dance celebration. They do it for all sorts of occasions. I'm betting it's because of your arrival." He smiled, showing even, white teeth.

Carmen nodded and smiled, wondering at it and not liking the way the man was hovering. "Jose," she called to one of her men that was passing. "My things can be unloaded in that house over there," she nodded towards where Maria was heading with her children. "Please have the men check on my babies," she added, and he smiled. He saluted her as he hurried away, directing one of the wagons to the house Maria had disappeared into.

"Your babies?" Harold asked, trying to be amiable.

"My horses," she returned as she walked off the main house porch and headed for the house where her children had disappeared. She found that it had two bedrooms and would be fine for a while, but it wouldn't be big enough for the long-term. "Maria, the men will be here soon with my furniture. Some will have to be stored in the barns until I can figure out what I'm going to do here."

"You will have to warn the children against going under the houses until we've made sure they are clear of spiders and snakes," Harold told her warningly, proving he had followed her.

Carmen was irked, but she nodded to show she understood, looking at Maria warningly. "Thank you, Cousin Harold. I appreciate your concern and consideration," she said sweetly. "We are going to have to discuss with Mr. Lawrence what his plans are and divide up the supplies he purchased as well as the sheep."

"How set is he on keeping his half of the sheep?" Harold asked as Carmen returned to the front porch of the house and looked around. The different angle gave her a panoramic view, and she could see why someone had settled in this area. It must be beautiful after the rains. Right now, it looked parched and dead but still pretty in its own way.

"The sheep were Mr. Lawrence's idea. I have no intention of cheating him out of anything," she informed her cousin frostily.

"No, no. I just thought perhaps, he would like to do a trade. Some of our sheep for a share of his Merinos," he amended hastily. Damn, she was prickly and beautiful in her ire.

"We could ask, but I own half that flock, and if four thousand Merinos aren't enough on our station, then how many would be enough?" she asked.

"Well, all would be welcome, and intermixed with our sheep, we should get ahead in a few years."

"A few years?" she turned from where she was observing the activity on the station. "How did you intend to buy me out?"

"Well, over time or with a bank loan," he began weakly.

"I think there is some misunderstanding here, cousin Harold," she began briskly as she saw Fabiola come up. "You don't own this land," she gestured at the hills around the home paddock. "You couldn't get a loan on it. From the few sheep I saw on the land, I take it you've had some setbacks?"

"We have," Fabiola answered for her brother, drawing Carmen's full attention. She looked at the woman hard. From what her uncle had written, both Fabiola and Harold were the result of his partner's, no real relation, liaison with an aboriginal woman. In her cousin Harold's case, he looked white, but had a weak chin and characteristics she could see wouldn't serve either a white man or an aboriginal man well. In the case of Fabiola, she saw that she was large boned, although not as large as Mel, and feminine in appearance. Her skin tone defined her as an Aborigine, and from what Carmen had experienced herself, she probably would not be welcome in Sydney. People frowned on mixing

the races. Even her Spanish heritage was suspect because her and her vaqueros were darker skinned than the English. The Hispanics looked nothing like the aboriginal people in bone structure. "We had fires that wiped out our flocks in the southern paddocks. Set by fossickers, who were mucking about with no care other than their own. Drought has taken a toll on our remaining flocks, but we are anticipating the rains, and with the influx of your flock, we should do better. You're right. We'd never get a loan, and I'm grateful you're here to help. Are your men staying, or are they heading back to the Americas?"

"They're staying," she informed her cousin, impressed despite her first impression of Harold.

"Then, they'll be expected to work," she stated.

"Yes, that was the plan. I was uncertain what we'd find here, but I'm willing and able to work," Carmen promised.

Fabiola's eyes sparkled. They had reached an understanding, and she sensed her *cousin* was of the same ilk, a strong woman bred for country such as this. "What kind of station is Mr. Lawrence planning on setting up?"

"I was hoping we might convince Mr. Lawrence to be one of our neighbors, if there is land available and it's something you could recommend?"

"How about we go out in a few of the paddocks tomorrow. We can take our men some supplies, and I can show you around the place?"

"That would be a good idea," Harold seconded the idea and Carmen saw the look in Fabiola's eye before she glanced at the brother and back to the tall woman.

"Or would you like to rest a few days?" She glanced behind Carmen to where the children were making themselves at home in the house, already running about and being followed by the faithful Maria.

"No, I'm used to traveling now, but let's go discuss it with Mel Lawrence and see what…he has to say about it." Her hesitation was only brief, but she wondered if Fabiola had caught it as her eyes flared slightly.

After Carmen's wagons were unloaded into her chosen house and some stalls in the barn, the rest were covered and placed away from the animals. The Hispanic men pitched in to help unload the rest of the supplies into the storage shed and elsewhere. Fabiola was pleased at the additional help as everyone, including Carmen and Mel, pitched in to not only unload the supply wagons but to stack the large bags of wool, so the wagons could immediately turn around the next day and head back to civilization with their crop.

CHAPTER SEVEN

They headed out the next day. Fabiola led the way, followed by Carmen and Mel and several packhorses. Only two of the vaqueros accompanied them to guard the senora. It had taken Mel several tries before Alinta understood that she was to stay in the house with all the supplies. She had been curious about the place, never having been in one of these structures before, but she took the job of *protecting* Mel's things seriously.

Fabiola explained they had split the paddocks up into sections to keep track of them, and a stockman oversaw each section, sometimes helped by an assistant, called a jackaroo here in Australia.

Mel and Carmen looked avidly about the land as Fabiola explained, pointing with her short whip to different features of the landscape.

"My father wanted to enclose all the paddocks, but he was too ambitious, and it never got done. Your uncle enclosed the paddocks to the south, but we ran out of money before we could do more, and those are now gone with the fires."

"This is a lot of land to enclose," Carmen commented.

"It is a lot of land, but it won't graze as many sheep as it would in England. Do they have sheep in America?" she asked, directing her question to them both.

"Oh, yes, and as it's a new land, it too has its problems in enclosing large areas to keep the animals contained."

Mel smiled. Carmen was using big words again, and she could tell that Fabiola was a little intimidated, even if she tried not to let it show. The woman was all bravado on social items but was brilliant when it came to the land and stock. She herself could learn a lot from the woman. She was still trying to figure the brother out. He seemed to always allow his sister to take the lead. He had stayed behind, ostensibly to supervise at the home paddock while his sister was gone.

She showed them a little valley, which was a bit greener than their own valley where the first flock was located. The dogs were trained not to bark, so as they rode into the valley, they started moving about restlessly instead, telling the stockman that something or someone was nearby. He looked up and waved when he saw them, curious about the people with Fabiola.

"John Neighbors, this is Uncle Jude's niece, Mrs. Carmen Pearson, and she's come here all the way from America," she told him.

John nodded. "Aye, we've been waiting on you for a while now," he said with a decided Irish brogue.

"Waiting on me?" Carmen asked.

"News that you weren't going to sell was all over our station. There is little to talk about here," Fabiola explained. "Anything of news about the family or the station owners is news to everyone here."

Carmen nodded, understanding. "I'm pleased to meet you, John," she stated. "This is Mel Lawrence, also of America. He is planning on setting up a station himself."

"How do you do?" the man said, holding out his hand.

Mel shook it, amused but trying not to show it. Mel found it ironic that this man would shake another man's hand and not offer to shake the hand of the station owner simply because she was a woman.

"Where's your hut?" Fabiola asked, not willing to waste time chin wagging.

He pointed it out to her and saluted as she started off, the two packhorses following her. He admired the horse that Carmen was riding, but he admired the woman more. Mel was amused when she saw him looking at the beautiful Hispanic woman. She turned her face away before he could see her amusement and be embarrassed by it. He did lose his smile when the two men he hadn't been introduced to glared with resentment towards him as they rode past.

The camp was set up with a bark hut. It was obviously not a long-term arrangement, but Fabiola got down, and the other two helped her measure out portions of peas, rice, coffee, salt, and other supplies. As they got back on their horses and headed east, she explained that each of the stockmen got an equal share, and she or one of her men visited them once every few weeks to ensure that nothing untoward had happened to them since there were dangers from flood, fire, and wild animals. Each stockman was supplied with a musket and other tools, and their job was to keep the sheep in good feed and alive. It required moving them every so often, so they didn't eat down to the roots and kept the available graze healthy in the paddocks.

"Dingoes are the greatest danger, and if you are going into an area where there have never been any sheep, they are going to be a problem," Fabiola explained, directing her comments to Mel.

Mel nodded. She had expected that and planned for it. She had picked up new guns in Sydney, disappointed that the muskets seemed so old and wishing for repeating rifles like those she had seen in the Americas. She'd already written to suppliers she knew of, but it would take a long time to get rifles sent to Australia and all the way to the station, if they even made it that far before they were stolen.

"I'm planning on shearing my sheep here at Twin Station," she explained to Fabiola when asked about her plans. "We can arrange supplies from here."

"I've already got my suppliers sending me supplies," Fabiola told her, frowning at the wording.

"If we increase our supplies and bring in larger orders, we can take advantage of quantity discounts and use the same drayage companies that you already have set up. I won't be in a position to have a drayage company haul in supplies and take away my wool clip for a couple years."

Fabiola nodded, understanding. It was obvious this man had thought things out, and the fact that Carmen was nodding meant they had discussed it. She was surprised how close the two Americans friends had become, but she supposed it was only understandable since they were from the same country. She didn't realize how vast America was, just as the two Americans hadn't realized how big Australia was.

They traveled east for hours and came across another stockman, going through introductions again as Fabiola measured out the supplies. They headed south after that and spent the night with the third stockman, who welcomed the owners and their guests. The variety of visitors provided a welcome respite from the monotony of his existence.

"I heard dingoes last night," he confided. "If someone could watch my flock, I'd hunt those bastards."

"I'll watch them, but I'd rather hunt with you," Mel offered as they sat around the fire, the dogs panting as they lay about between the hut and the fold the sheep were kept in while waiting to be fed. The fold was made up of split rail fencing, and the sheep had settled down inside it.

"You think you could find your way back to the station?" Fabiola asked, looking at Mel speculatively.

"Yep, your home ranch…er, station is back that way, and as we haven't hit the track that we came in on yet, it must be south and west of here," she said, pointing in the proper directions.

Fabiola was impressed. The Outback could quickly become disorienting. She was also pleased that Carmen didn't seem to be put out by the vastness of the land. "Then why don't you stay and help him," she nodded to the stockman. "If you want, you can try to catch up with us or meet us back at the station."

Mel agreed and found herself watching the stockman's sheep the next day. The dogs were confused by a different human giving them commands, but they were well-trained and took the sheep out to where the stockman said he had been heading. She heard no sounds of shooting but saw the slinking forms of what looked like dogs late in the day as she took the sheep to water at the creek. She waited until they were headed back to the fold before cocking and firing at the animals when she spotted one in the brush. The howl of pain was cut off abruptly, and she hoped it died quickly. She quickly reloaded, her horse nervous from the noise of the gun, but she held it in check, then reloaded the empty barrel, pleased she wasn't unprotected as there had been a second barrel, just in case.

That night, she cooked her own meal, making pan biscuits, or as they called them here, damper and peas. She wondered where the stockman had gotten to. The next morning, she found out when she saw smoke rising from a hillside miles away from her own position. He rode in on his horse late in the morning and explained he had found the dingoes' den. He'd blocked all the entrance holes he could find, and then he started fires in the lower holes to smoke them out and smother them in their own den. He explained that the den was connected by tunnels, and when he discovered one hole he had missed, he clubbed the escaping dingoes, blocking the hole with their bodies to stop the others from escaping. He took great pride in his achievement. Mel was sickened but didn't show it. She saddled her horse up, went back to the fire and gathered her things, and headed out. She felt there was no need to stay another day.

Mel headed south some more until she came to the track they had ridden in on, then headed west on it. It took her the rest of the day, but she arrived at the station with no problems, putting her horse in the corral and heading back to the house she had been assigned. Alinta was relieved to see her return.

CHAPTER EIGHT

Alinta didn't understand these white people. As they headed west in the direction where her father and mother had lived, she hoped to find some sign of them. She was depressed when they went by the same area and there was nothing to see; too much time had passed. They continued down the endless track, but she knew she was far from her tribe's hunting grounds, and she wasn't certain she would have been welcomed back anyway. Mel was so nice to her, and she knew all she could do was learn his ways and hope he would want to keep her. She began to suspect that Mel was not what he seemed. In fact, she was almost certain that Mel wasn't a man at all. Her tribe, all tribes in fact, had revered people like that, who had a spirit of the opposite sex living inside them. She understood this, and it didn't bother her, but she didn't discuss it with Mel since Mel hadn't brought it up. There was also the language barrier, and while she was with Bradley, she hadn't bothered to learn any words in their language. With Mel encouraging her and helping her to learn, she felt the need to communicate.

When they arrived at the station, there was a flurry of activity, but Mel made sure she understood that the house was for them to use. She further emphasized that by bringing in their supplies from the packhorses and wagons, then laying their beds side by side in one of the rooms. Alinta had never seen a bed, and she was confused when Mel placed their bedrolls on top of these structures. Mel slept on it one night, so Alinta understood, but on the nights when Mel wasn't there, she took her bedroll and slept on the hard floor.

The Aborigines, who had a small village on the creek, stared at Alinta curiously as she learned where to fetch the meat to feed their dogs. The dogs stayed under the house, but only because Mel had ordered them to. Each would come out only to squat or lift its leg. The feces were building up, and the flies were terrible. One of the Aborigines came and showed Alinta what a shovel was for. Alinta was unable to speak her tribe's language, but by pantomiming, the Aborigine was able to explain how to bury the feces or throw them far from the home paddock. Alinta understood and took her duty seriously. She was caring for Mel's possessions, and the responsibility weighed heavily on her shoulders. She was worried about Mel returning, so although she was given food, she rooted through her master's possessions looking for additional food she knew she could eat. She was relieved when Mel returned late in the day just a few days later.

"How are you feeling?" Mel asked upon seeing the woman.

"Fine," she admitted. She had learned a lot, but this was one of the few words she truly knew the meaning of.

"Baby making you sick?" Mel asked, concerned and hoping that the woman had rested. She saw how neat and orderly the supplies were in the house and wondered. She had made it clear weeks ago on the long trip out here that she understood Alinta was with child.

"Baby fine," she said, rubbing her rounding belly.

"Good, good," Mel said, nodding. She had to be careful not to talk down to the woman. She didn't know much English, and she saw that the Australians tended to treat Aborigines like children, singsonging their speech to them and keeping it abrupt and basic, as though these people didn't have much intelligence. She knew that Alinta was smart. Still, she sought out Harold and asked him if any of the Aborigines in the village could come and talk to Alinta.

Several tried, and using gestures Mel could have made herself, they her helped *speak* to Alinta and ask her what she wanted. She needed to know if Alinta wished to stay with Mel or go back to her own people.

"They won't want her back, Mr. Mel," one of the aboriginal men explained to Mel. "Most people no want back woman they give away to white man."

"They didn't give her away though, she was taken," Mel argued, having learned that when she had gambled with Bradley for the young woman.

"Still, they no want her back," the man said and then pantomimed to Alinta, who shook her head sadly.

Between the aboriginal pantomime and the little English Alinta understood, she was saddened. "Mr. Mel no want me?" she finally asked.

"I want you," Mel stated clearly. "If you want to go with me, you can. If you want to go back to your family, you can. If you want to stay here, you can. It's your decision." She understood Alinta's hesitation now as she tried to make herself understood.

"Alinta's decision?"

Mel nodded, smiling encouragingly.

"I go you?"

"Only if you want, but I'll be roaming, and that won't be good for your baby," she told her honestly, wondering how much she understood. She was fond of the young woman, but it wouldn't be fair to take her with her. Although Mel had originally planned to be alone, she would be lonely without the young woman, but the thought of the woman giving birth out here was something she didn't consider.

"You want Alinta go you?" she asked, and the Aborigine gestured some more, relaying the message and making himself understood. Here in the white man's station, men were to be obeyed, and the Aborigine was becoming exasperated with the white Yank man for giving the young aboriginal woman a choice. Did he understand how big a decision that was?

"Yes, but only if Alinta wants to go with me," Mel responded, hoping she understood it was a choice and not a command.

"Alinta want go with Mel," she said imperfectly, looking relieved.

Mel smiled, nodding, and Harold, who had watched, amused, nodded to the aboriginal elder, who had tried to interpret for them. Mel wasn't sure if the man had helped or not. She thanked him, and Harold sent him on his way.

"So, you are going to take the woman as your own?" he asked, sounding almost insinuating.

"No, she isn't *my own*," she objected. "She is my friend, and she's welcome to come with me while I search for a place of my own. She was born here, but I feel as though I belong too. Maybe we can find a place together."

He nodded, having been born here and knowing no other place. He left them alone and waited for Carmen and his sister to return, wondering if his sister had relayed their plans to their cousin.

CHAPTER NINE

Mel was also waiting for Carmen and Fabiola to return. She had help from the blacksmith to tighten the shoes on her horses, watching and learning how they did some of the blacksmithing. She checked on the large flock of sheep that a couple men were taking out on the hills surrounding the home paddock, so the grass nearby wouldn't wear down from overeating.

She packed, and repacked the supplies she had in the house, checking against future need. She had given a list for the carters to take back to Sydney to order her own supplies. She included a letter, which instructed her bank to draw from her account to pay for the supplies. She also wrote to her solicitor explaining where she was and instructing him to check up on the dressmaker's shop for her. Another letter went to her accountant making the same request. A third letter went directly to the shop, asking Mrs. Waters how she was doing after all these months. She knew it might be a year before she heard from any or all of them. Meanwhile, she was making plans.

Carmen and Fabiola returned, and the supplies on the packhorses were gone. Another of the men left the next day to finish the rounds on the other side of the station as they had only gone through half of the flocks surrounding their station. They were spread out, but not nearly as large as they were before the losses Twin Station had suffered.

The four of them ate dinner together, discussing where Mel should head out and establish her own station. While Fabiola would have liked Mel to the south where there weren't any of their own flocks since the fire, Mel was drawn north based on conversations with the stockmen they had visited as well as those working at the home paddock.

"I wish to find my own place," Mel asserted, and Carmen understood her desire, but Fabiola and her brother both tried to convince her that the southern paddocks were empty of sheep and would be to her benefit. "There's more people there too," she pointed out. "I appreciate what you are saying," Mel addressed Fabiola and ignored Harold since he didn't contribute much of value to the conversation. He mostly sat gazing at Carmen, who also ignored him as she joined in the conversation.

"You wouldn't be like a tenant farmer," Carmen pointed out. "If you go north, you will totally be on your own if something happens. How are you going to deal with Alinta's pregnancy?" she asked.

"I guess we will be going slower than I thought," she admitted. "It will give me a chance to scope out the land and choose where I'll set up my station."

"As far as I know, there are no stations north of here," Fabiola conceded since the Yank was so determined to go. "East of here there are a few, as I'm sure you saw on the tracks, but nothing like on the other side of the Cobdogla."

Mel smiled, loving the Aborigine word for the renamed Darling River. She only knew that because of the endless conversations on the long trip out here. "I expect it to be that way for my lifetime," she agreed. She sounded eminently satisfied with that idea, preferring to be off and alone. Some of the men on the way out here had gotten quieter with the Outback pressing in on them, a phenomenon Foster and other men had said deeply affected some, while others could handle the oppressive silence of the Outback. Mel and Carmen, from what she had seen, were freed by it. None of the vaqueros had been affected, only the men in the drays bringing the supplies out. Not all of them, of course, but enough that it had been noticed.

They discussed what she should look for and what she would need. Carmen had agreed to keep some of Mel's many supplies here on the station, and she would start up in a couple of months to resupply her and check on their progress. Fabiola raised an eyebrow at this plan, wondering again at the relationship between the Yank and her cousin. As far as she could ascertain, they were merely friends. She'd been surprised that the vaqueros allowed her cousin out of their sight but saw that they trusted the Yank. The remaining Californians hadn't been pleased by Mel returning without the Hispanic woman. Fabiola had been impressed that her cousin was able to handle herself, using a whip and a pistol without flinching as they traveled along. Her bodyguards hadn't been necessary. Their conversations had been about the land, and Fabiola explained what they had done in the years since her own father had passed. Her mother had died giving birth to her weak brother, and her father and uncle had both raised the children, teaching them their letters, making sure they spoke and wrote English, and teaching them how to run the station. In due course, the station had grown, but fires and drought had wiped out nearly half of it, and even now, they were rebuilding their flocks. The death of first, her father, then, her uncle, combined with the fires to the south, had been an additional setback to the isolated station.

Now, her cousin was adding this man to their supply route? Fabiola listened as they discussed things that Mel might need or should look for but found herself surprised and appreciative as the Yank and her cousin included her in their conversation. They felt her advice was invaluable since she had lived out here all her life.

"But you've never gone that far north?" Mel asked the woman.

Fabiola shook her head. "There's always been too much work here on the station that needed tending. Why would I go up there when I'm needed here?"

"Curiosity?" Mel asked with a smile, teasing her and pleased when she returned the smile.

"Perhaps," she agreed, surprised to find herself smiling back at the Yank and wondering about him. There was something not quite right there, but she had yet to think about it deeply. There were too many other things occupying her mind after her cousin's arrival. Thinking her cousin would be manageable and amenable to their plans; she had been pleasantly surprised and found the challenge to be agreeable and work out their differences of how the station should be run was quite pleasurable. Fabiola and Harold owned half the station, but if they couldn't agree, the other half was owned by this cousin, who could

outvote them. If their plan to have this cousin marry Harold came to fruition, that would negate her half vote, and there would be just two votes instead of three. Harold, for the most part, was agreeable to any and all of Fabiola's plans, letting her run the station as she saw fit, but it had been his idea to get this unknown cousin of theirs to marry him. After meeting Carmen, he was even more enthused by his idea, but Fabiola wondered if her cousin was attracted to this Yank?

Mel found herself working with the various men, Carmen, and Fabiola as they separated out the sheep, making sure that most of the Merinos she was taking were the three- and four-year-olds they had agreed upon.

Mel asked Fabiola about a saddle for Alinta, and they found one in one of the storage sheds, an old sidesaddle that was in desperate need of care. Mel spent several evenings rubbing tallow into the worn leather as they got ready, bringing a shine to it as it absorbed the grease. After buying a bridle, she rubbed this too until it was supple, and the leather was ready to use. She saddled one of her Brumbies that she had used as a packhorse and taught Alinta how to ride. She seemed steady, sitting sideways on the horse as Mel patiently showed her how to use the reins on the beast. Alinta wondered, seeing Mel ride her horse with her legs on both sides of it but hesitated to question the situation as she sensed this was important to Mel.

Readying her packs on the remaining horses, Mel checked and rechecked the house for their things, then whistled to her dogs and hoisted Alinta up on the waiting horse before gathering up her own reins and stepping into the saddle. Alinta led the remaining packhorses, but fortunately for the unschooled rider, her horse chose to follow Mel's, which made it easier for her to control the beast. They headed for the holding pens where the four thousand sheep Mel was taking were waiting. Carmen, Fabiola, and several of Carmen's men were coming along for the ride to the edge of the station, using this opportunity to familiarize Carmen with more of the land she had inherited. Mel appreciated their help as her dogs brought the flock out of the pens, and they began their trek. It took two days to get to the edge of the property or rather, the grazing areas that Twin Station claimed.

An odd set of domed hills was at the northernmost line, and Fabiola pointed it out as they pushed the flock up to the top of one and let the dogs and the sheep slow on the far side. The sheep immediately slowed to graze the long and untouched grasses. "Well, from here you can choose your station," she said as she viewed the land from their vantage point. "I don't know of anyone else claiming the land, but you'll have to fight dingoes, snakes, boars, and weather. Watch for fires and other things as well." She wasn't telling the Yank anything he didn't already know or anything they hadn't already discussed, but he looked kind of eager to be off. She glanced at the aboriginal woman who followed him on her own horse and realized the horse was stopping only because Mel had stopped and not because of the woman's prowess at riding. She looked slightly ill, her stomach making it obvious that she was pregnant. Fabiola wondered if the

woman would lose the child with all the traveling Mel planned to do as he scouted the territory he was going to claim.

"I thank you for your advice," Mel said and looked eagerly to the other side of the domed hills, glancing at Carmen with a smile of delight. As far as any of them knew, the land before them was uncharted territory. It was still quite arid, but soon, the autumn rains would be coming on. The sheep had grown coats in the months it took to get out to the station and soon, they would be giving birth. The rams she had chosen were among the ewes now, but she hoped to keep them separate once her station was established. "I guess this is goodbye," she said to the Hispanic woman, smiling her thanks for the friendship they had shared.

"No, it is goodbye for now. I told you, I'll be looking for you to bring you some of your supplies. Don't get lost," she teased, a smile on her beautiful face.

Mel looked at her friend's face, wishing for something that had never been there but pleased that the friendship had come about despite her attraction to the woman. She glanced at Fabiola, sensing her admiration for the same woman. That was a surprise. She had seen Harold looking hopefully and almost foolishly at their cousin, and she knew Carmen was nothing but polite to the man, not encouraging him in the least. "Well, we will see you then," she said as she gathered her reins and urged her horse forward, Alinta following.

Carmen watched her friend as she followed the large flock of sheep, her dogs doing an excellent job of keeping the sheep moving slowly, so they could graze. She was pleased that she had been able to sell Mel a few of the dogs she had purchased back in Sydney since they worked so well together, and her cousins had more than enough. She'd kept the three best for breeding, but the others had gone with her friend to keep the large flock in order.

"You will see him again," Fabiola promised, glancing at the vaqueros that had accompanied them.

"Of course, I will. Mel is a unique individual and will succeed at anything…he takes on." The hesitation was infinitesimal, but Fabiola noted it. She'd noticed several times when her cousin had hesitated over certain words and wondered if it was the way Hispanics spoke in America. She didn't think so.

They waited until Mel reached the tree line, turned back to wave to them all, and then disappeared. Her sheep appeared beyond the tree line a while later, white specks against the greenery, but they didn't see the two women or their horses, and it was time to turn back.

"I'll take you and show you our northwest border," Fabiola promised her cousin as they began to make their way off the odd dome-shaped hills.

CHAPTER TEN

Mel felt a tremendous rush to be alone, *completely* alone in the Outback. The responsibility for so many sheep weighed heavily on her shoulders, but they were hers. If they lived or died, it was on her. She could afford the loss, but the idea of losing was an antithesis to her. She would succeed. She knew it was a lot of work, but she eagerly anticipated it. Slowly, she became aware that she wasn't alone, not truly alone. Alinta was with her as well as the horses and dogs. They were all depending on her, and she would make sure they were all taken care of. She glanced at Alinta, wondering why the woman had chosen to go with her. She was grateful for the company but worried that the woman felt some sort of obligation to her for freeing her from the chains Bradley had put on her.

She let the dogs move the sheep through the woods to a meadow on the far side. The sheep had slowed to eat, eager to consume the grass and twigs that Fabiola had explained was called saltbrush, which was excellent for sheep to graze upon as well as the mallee seed. Not familiar with many of the plants, Mel knew she had to rely on what people had told her as well her own innate good sense. Allowing the sheep to graze as they walked along, she spotted a deeper green as they climbed another hill, the brush on the far side keeping them from easily holding the flock there, so she had the dogs skirt it and head for that deeper green. Finding a pond, or what they called a billabong, with a spring in it was a delightful surprise. This water would be invaluable to a paddock, and Mel watered the sheep, dogs, and horses well before allowing them to fall to cropping the grass.

"We'll make camp here," she told Alinta as she let the horses drink their fill and then went to the far side, a little ways away from the water, so the wild animals that lived here could still make their way to it.

Mel showed Alinta how to hobble the horses, so they could still graze but couldn't wander too far away from the camp. Together, they gathered wood, Alinta using her walking stick to turn some of the wood before picking it up. Mel was sickened when the woman ate the grubs she found but turned away, feeling it was none of her business. When they had a good supply of wood by their camp, Mel began to drag longer poles, and Alinta understood she intended to build a hut. She proved useful as she wove the branches into a roof that would shed rain. Mel was pleased because it proved they were compatible to work together.

Mel took some of the straight poles and used them to make a fold, stringing rope around them and herding her flock into it. She knew it didn't really hold the sheep, but they thought it did, and she shuddered to think what would happen if they broke out of it. Still, if she didn't lose many sheep, these were the start of many flocks she hoped to raise. She knew they wouldn't all be Merinos, but she had a good start and hoped to arrange to buy more in the coming years, but to do that, she would need to hire stockmen and jackaroos, and she wasn't ready for that yet. She called the dogs, who eagerly followed her back to the camp, sitting down and patiently waiting as they panted and watched.

Mel started a fire and began to teach Alinta how to cook again. She had tried on the trip out here, but the presence of so many others seemed to intimidate the Aborigine, who had been nervous. Now, with just the two of them, she seemed more willing to try, and she was eager to please Mel.

The sheep settled down in their makeshift fold, and Mel hung the carcass she had been using on a tree to get it off the ground and out of their way. She pulled the bag from around it in order to cut slices of mutton for their dinner and the dogs'. The animals whined appreciatively in anticipation. She showed Alinta what she was doing and allowed her to use the knife, which seemed to surprise and please the young woman. She was still in awe of this white man's stone, and she realized it was sharper than any stone she had ever chipped to cut things. When Mel gave her one of her own including a sheath, she held it reverently.

"Careful there," Mel cautioned as the sharpness seemed to fascinate the woman, and she wondered what kind of tools the aboriginal people used. She could only imagine they were primitive.

While cooking the meat, rice, peas, and damper in pots on the fire, the peace was shattered only by an occasional bird squawking as the sun went down and settled in for the night. Mel sighed blissfully, leaning back against a large log that reflected the heat of the fire into the small hut they had built. She was pleased that Alinta had helped her, probably making it better than the Yank would have with her woven branches. It was done none too soon. It looked like rain was coming, something she had been expecting. As the sun set and the shadows moved in on them, Mel looked up to see a stunning sight. Alinta was silhouetted against the backdrop of the Outback, looking fit and beautiful. Her crinkly, aboriginal hair looked brushed out as a slight breeze had it floating about the woman. Mel's gasp startled them both, and Alinta looked at her. She wondered if Mel saw something she hadn't, but they both knew the native woman's senses were much keener than the American's. For the first time, Mel didn't see Alinta as the aboriginal woman she was or the slave woman she had been. Instead, she saw a vibrantly alive and healthy woman, who stole her breath away. She finally looked down at the meat she was burning, turning it to cook the other side, so it would be even. She fussed with the pans, and Alinta moved to help her, eager to learn how to cook food the way Mel liked it.

Mel hadn't considered the young woman unattractive, and she didn't notice her skin color. Instead, she felt sorry for her and the situation she found herself in. She hadn't considered that the woman might think of as her master to be obeyed. When Alinta had chosen not to seek out her people, something Mel still didn't quite understand, she was pleased she wanted to go with her into the unknown. It wasn't just the companionship. She felt genuine affection for this woman she had

taken responsibility for. She had never thought she was attracted to her, but tonight's view had shown her that Alinta was a vibrantly attractive woman, and she looked at her differently now. The bulge of her baby was barely noticeable, and even that made the woman more attractive. Mel glanced at her repeatedly, trying not to make it obvious.

Alinta was aware of a change in Mel. She knew Mel was looking at her the same way she was looking at *him*. She wondered if Mel would ever admit she was a woman, and she wondered why she chose to pass herself off as a man. She didn't have the words to ask yet, and even when she did, she probably wouldn't ask, knowing it was a personal choice. She was puzzled by many things the white people did but was eager to learn their ways now that she couldn't go back to her own people. The Aborigines she had met back at Twin Station had tried to communicate, and while there were the rudiments in order to make themselves known, there had been a subtle difference that went beyond language between them and Alinta. She didn't understand it, but when she thought Mel didn't want her to come with her, she had been panicked. Finally, she was appeased when she realized Mel did want her. It had never occurred to her that Mel was giving her a choice. She didn't understand that it was *her* choice. She hoped that Mel would be her mate now that she was far from Bradley and men like him. She would do everything in her power to be the best mate she could be to Mel. She would learn everything Mel would teach her, and perhaps, someday, Mel would tell her that she wanted her to be her mate. In the meantime, she would show she was willing to do whatever Mel wanted of her. For now, that consisted of learning to cook.

It wasn't difficult to make their food, to feed the dogs, and to tend the fire. Mel made a circle of the flock, walking slowly, her pistol at her waist and her double-barreled musket in her hand as she looked for the dingoes she heard yipping in the dark. It was past the time they normally did their evening hunting but not so late that they weren't a danger. She knew Alinta understood the word dingo and knew Mel was protecting the sheep against them. She was a little uncomfortable around Alinta now that she knew she felt an attraction for her. She tried to hide it as they returned from their walk and bedded down for the night, their ground sheets below their bedrolls that were rolled out side by side in the hut.

Mel smoked her pipe a little before she took out a stick and made a mark on it with her knife. This would ensure she wouldn't forget the days. She knew the date when she arrived on her land, or what she hoped would be her land, and by marking the stick daily, she hoped the timelessness of the Outback wouldn't lull her into forgetting important dates. She would have to take the sheep in for shearing, but that time was months away, well after they gave birth. Finally, she could delay going to bed no longer, so she banked the fire, hoping the rain wouldn't come and put it out. She headed into the hut, Alinta quietly following as they got ready for bed. Mel removed her boots, hanging them upside down on a stick she had pushed into the dirt, hoping that would keep out any critters that crawled or slithered. Her stockinged feet felt the relief of being out of the tight confines of leather, but the boots fit well now, and she had another pair for when these wore out. She removed her pants and her short summer underwear with its flap, something she hadn't allowed anyone but Alinta to see. Her shirt hung down her thighs, and she would sleep in that. She glanced at the brown-haired woman to see if she was watching.

Alinta slept in the shirt that Mel had given her. She wore it all day like a long dress and didn't change it. It was due to be washed, and Mel would insist on that in the coming days when she washed her own clothes. It wasn't like Alinta didn't have other shirts or clothes, and Mel couldn't stand some odors. She hoped to convince the native woman to bathe, but she didn't quite know how to approach this as she hadn't bathed in months either, instead settling for spritz baths from basins of water or a bucket.

In all the months they had been together, even in the house, they had never been so aware of sleeping side by side, but tonight, Mel was tense. She wasn't aware that Alinta also sensed the tension, although she didn't quite understand it. Mel tried to think of all the work she had to do to establish her station and hoped she was up to it. She was trying to concentrate on those thoughts instead of thinking of the picture in her mind of the firm bodied young woman beside her, lying just inches away from her.

Alinta didn't understand it as attraction, but she knew she wanted to touch Mel and be held by her. She had been held by her at various times, but for some reason she craved it now. She wondered at that but didn't think about it much as she fell into a dreamless sleep.

Mel was pleased when she heard the other woman sleeping next to her and turned onto her side, trying to peer at her in the faint light from the fire. All she saw was shadow and silhouette, but she didn't mind. The picture burnt into her head from that evening was something she would cherish forever. She didn't even realize as she too drifted off, tired from the days of traveling and all they had yet to do.

CHAPTER ELEVEN

Mel was up early the next morning, eager to start on all the work she had waiting. The rains had held off, but the clouds were threatening. She built up the fire but didn't have to start breakfast as Alinta saw that as her duty and had begun to heat up the damper and fry some leftover meat from the night before. Mel took a moment to take care of her business, holding the musket in one hand while she balanced, then using the paper she had brought along to wipe herself before covering it all in dirt. She then continued towards the flock. The sheep were getting up and beginning to graze as the daylight brightened. The sun wouldn't make a full appearance that day with the clouds gathering and indicating rain, but for now, it was holding off, and for that, Mel was grateful as she laid out her work.

The dogs stirred restlessly, greeting her but doing their duty and watching the sheep. She greeted each one individually, praising them. This was something she knew other grazers didn't do, but she thought she got more work out of her own dogs with kindness. She was appreciative of the extra dogs Carmen had sold her, knowing she might have need of them at some point as she started out with her flock in these virgin lands. She had heard the dingoes the night before and wasn't surprised when the one of the dogs indicated something was about. She walked slowly, trying not to alarm the sheep as she skirted the perimeter of her fold. On the far side, she saw eyes peeking out at her in the early dawn. It was an excellent time for the wild dogs to teach their young how to hunt. She didn't hesitate, firing the musket at the eyes. She heard yelping, and when she spotted another dingo that made to slink away, she fired the second barrel, hitting this one too. She wondered if she should take a leaf out of the stockman's book and find their den in order to destroy them. She knew the two she had killed weren't the whole pack and there had to be more. She quickly reloaded both barrels, knowing it was foolish to have an unloaded gun in hand at any time.

The sound of the gun in the early morning air startled the sheep, but the dogs kept them at bay. Alinta had looked up at the sound of the thunder stick, afraid of it from the first time she heard it on her journey. She didn't touch it, and Mel hadn't offered to show it to her. She watched as Mel returned, and she hurried to finish preparing her breakfast, having learned to place the food on the tin plates with a fork and knife. She occasionally looked at the man stone, which is what she called the metal her father had coveted so much he had been willing to put his family in danger. Her life would have been completely different

if he had never heard that other man's tale or seen the products of his trade before starting out to find his own. She realized now, he had nothing he could have traded to the white men. She wondered if the kangaroo he had hunted would have netted him anything? Those men were quite different from any others she had known. Even the ones Mel had been with were different: kinder and not looking at her in a lecherous way. She put those thoughts behind her. She was here with Mel and still wondering what they would do next.

After breakfast, Mel made sure to show her how to wash the dishes they had used, laying them on the rocks around their camp to dry, so they were ready to use again when lunch came around. Next, she let the sheep out of their makeshift fold and sent the dogs around the large flock, leading them out to graze in the big field near their camp. While the sheep grazed, she slung her musket to her back and brought her axe with her to chop down dead trees in the nearby woods. She also gathered any downed trees, and using the horses, roped the deadfall to transport them to a spot she had chosen. This is where she would build a permanent fold for the sheep.

Alinta was watching Mel and wanted to help, but Mel wouldn't let her lift the heavier trees. Worried about her pregnancy, Mel tried explaining her concerns. Alinta didn't quite understand but dutifully helped where she could. When Mel began to dig up some of the plants to replant around the large fold, she helped whenever Mel would allow her.

Mel used the split rails, deadfalls, and plants to build a sturdy wall and was able to get a portion of the fold done that day before having to move the sheep, so they wouldn't crop too much of the grass near their new camp too quickly. By the time she returned to the camp, Alinta had made lunch, or tiffin as they called it. Mel smiled at the differences between American and Australian phrases. She ate it gladly, having worked hard all morning and feeling appreciative of Alinta's contribution.

That night, the dingoes returned, and Mel was lucky enough to kill another, but the sheep were restless, and every noise had her leaping up, worried that they would break out of the rope fold. She was exhausted the next morning as she attempted to build more of the permanent fold. This continued during the next week or so as she built the sturdy fold. Once the sheep were inside the permanent fold, she finally got a good night's sleep. She took the time to wash herself and her dirty clothes in the billabong the next day as the sheep grazed. Trying to get Alinta to join her proved impossible, but she did convince her to change her shirt. Only after the weather turned colder and the rain finally came, was she able to convince Alinta to wear drawers, and eventually, she got her into the pants she had purchased for her so long ago.

The dingoes continued to attempt to get at the sheep, and Mel was forced to hunt for them. Leaving most of the dogs to guard the fold, she took Alinta and a couple dogs to hunt for the den. Alinta proved to be invaluable in this endeavor once she realized what Mel was looking for. She practically took her straight to the den, the holes nearly invisible against the dusky dirt around the rocks where the dingoes had dug. Knowing they would be back from hunting in the morning, she piled stones up around all the holes she could find. The dogs were eager, whining and wanting to dig at the holes. They smelled their nemeses, but Mel commanded them away. She and Alinta gathered

wood and dried grass and left them near the holes but not so near that the human smell would distract the wild dogs.

Early the next morning, leaving the hungry sheep in the fold, they hurried back to the den with several of the dogs and filled the holes with the rocks before starting a fire with the wood and grasses, then pushing them into the holes. Remembering the stockman's tale, she tried to duplicate his efforts, and this proved to be successful. The dingoes, tired from a night of hunting, tried to get out of their holes but were suffocated in the den. The dogs, agitated, would have dug them out and fought them, but Mel kept them away, and none of the dingoes from this den escaped.

The threat was now eliminated, and Mel strengthened her fold while the sheep were out of it during the day. It was large and could hold the entire flock. After a few days, she began to think about her plans for her station. She didn't want to overgraze the area around this fold, and with that in mind she scouted around and determined to head a few miles away and establish another permanent fold. They were again hunted by dingoes, but Mel was a good shot, and Alinta was as good as the dogs at sensing their presence. Now that she understood Mel wanted to kill them, Alinta was able to spot them and point them out to her. They eliminated another smaller den, this one with pups in it judging by the sounds. Mel's heart hurt at the thought of killing the young, but the young would grow up, and she couldn't afford to have them around with the sheep she intended to raise on these acres.

Mel had finished building her third fold when the rains began in earnest, causing the creeks to rise, making rivers overflow, and flooding out entire areas that were normally dry. Once arid areas were now lush and luxuriant with the growth that fed her animals. Some days, the sheep were all miserable as they cropped the grass in the rain, their wooly coats drenched and unable to dry out. Mel worried about the cold and disease that came with the rain. The sheep were hearty, although she'd lost a few to dingoes, one to a snake bite, and another to some plants that grew around the creek where she stopped one day.

Mel moved on despite the rains, always making sure to cross any creeks or rivers before settling in for the night. She had heard this was a good practice when she was in the western United States because you never knew what was upstream and might cause flooding downstream by morning. She used that idea here in Australia despite the different land, plants, and animals. The animals fascinated her, and she watched them while talking to Alinta. She wanted to know her language, but mainly she was teaching her the names of things she knew in English. The words kangaroo or wallaby were easy, even cockatoo or bird, but some of the animals Mel didn't know, and she had no one to ask out here. The learning wasn't one-sided. Alinta warned her about a snake, the worm-like twitching of its tail the only thing visible in the leaves as it tried to entice something to eat it, springing out to strike and kill whatever dared approach. Alinta sensed it and threw pebbles until it sprang up, attacked, then slithered off. Mel was amazed when her friend showed her things like this.

Alinta was astonished that Mel didn't know such ordinary things and was pleased to show her what she knew. The white man/woman had so many wonderous things and seemed to know so much, but Alinta could still teach her things she thought of as common, not realizing her parents had probably shown her long ago.

The rain continued, and Mel was surprised so much water could fall as she slowly got her fourth fold built. She realized she was really

honing her skills with the axe, and her muscles were building up in her arms. She felt fine, and their supplies were holding out much better than she had anticipated, mostly due to Alinta's scavenging for plants and fruits. She'd even convinced Mel to shoot a kangaroo, and it was delicious, a nice change from mutton.

The wethers Mel had taken provided skins that she stretched, using the roofs of their shelters to dry them as she scraped the fat from them. Foster had showed her how to do this back when she was learning that rubbing them with peppermint from the trees gave them a nice smell. She managed to stitch the hides together and make herself a stockman's coat with warm wool that kept her from the elements. She made a much smaller one for Alinta, who refused to wear it at first, but as the weather turned freezing cold and her bulk increased, she used it not only as a coat but as a blanket as well. The two women stayed warm in the sheepskin coats Mel made, which had also allowed her to show Alinta how to sew. They were heavy coats but rainproof and kept both women warm.

Carmen, Fabiola, and several stockmen including some of the vaqueros, followed the path the sheep took as they cropped their way across the range. Noting the fine, large, sturdy folds that Mel was constructing, they could see she was building with permanence in mind. It took them a while to find the two and their bulging flock.

Now curious about this land after Mel's teasing comments, Fabiola was eager to see this northern range. She realized it might even be better than the Twin Station range.

"Carmen!" Mel greeted her; the dogs having alerted her to the presence of strangers. She didn't think it was dingoes at this time of day, but the dogs had been agitated. She smiled greetings to the men accompanying the two women and greeted Fabiola by name, glancing at the many packhorses they had brought with them.

"Mel, that is quite a bit of land you've laid out for yourself. Intending to take over all of New South Wales?" Carmen teased after she had greeted her friend.

"I'm still looking for my home paddock," she admitted. "It's hard in this weather." And as she said that the rain continued to plunk down on her stockman's hat. Everyone was wearing similar attire.

"Hello, Alinta," the two women greeted the aboriginal woman, noting how pregnant she looked now as she sat sideways on her horse in her sheepskin coat while watching the sheep.

"Misses Carmen, Misses Fabiola," she said in reply, having trouble with the second names, which didn't come easily to her. She'd practiced, hearing Mel often talking about these two women admiringly.

"Alinta would you mind showing them where to put our supplies in the hut?" Mel asked her, making it her choice, but the eager young woman immediately set off on her horse, a couple of the men following behind her pulling the packhorses.

"She's gotten so big," Carmen commented when she was out of earshot.

Mel nodded. "I estimate she's due right after the sheep."

"That sounds like a lot of work," Fabiola mentioned, wondering how Mel was going to cope. She knew she wouldn't want to have a flock this big plus a pregnant woman to worry about.

"And two of my bitches are pregnant too," she lamented with a laugh at her situation, but it was of her own making. She should have held off letting the rams in among her sheep until later, but there was nothing she could have done about Alinta's due date. They were only guessing anyway. They had no idea when the carter had impregnated the poor woman.

Carmen laughed with her, and after a moment, Fabiola joined in. "Do you want me to send some of my men to help?" Carmen asked helpfully.

"You'll have enough to do with your own flocks to tend to. I knew what the work entailed before I set off on this adventure," Mel reminded her well-meaning friend.

"I'm sure you did," she consoled. "If you need–" she began, but Mel cut her off.

"Thank you."

"Damned independent cuss. We could send a couple–" Fabiola began exasperatedly.

"I know," she returned abruptly, sounding just as exasperated.

Carmen shook her head but laughed, so Fabiola wouldn't get angry. She knew Mel was independent, headstrong, and probably out to prove a point. Still, the land she had chosen was beautiful, and now, with the rains, she appreciated Twin Station even more. It had been brought to life, and the dismal, empty sections south of the station didn't look so bad with the growing grasses. They'd spread out their Merinos between the various flocks, hoping to interbreed them in the coming years as their flocks increased.

The women discussed the various sheep, and Mel could speak knowledgeably, having gleaned a lot from Foster and his men as well as the station owners and stockmen they had met on the trip out.

Both women were glad to help bring in the flock of sheep to the nearly finished fold that Mel had been building despite the winter rains. The rope stretched across on only two sides, but the sheep were relatively safe. Dinner was a grand affair as they continued their talk about stock. Mel further admitted two of her Brumby mares were in foal, probably due to Carmen's fine stallion covering them on the trip out, but fortunately for her, they weren't due for a while. Carmen and Fabiola had a good laugh over the burgeoning increases in Mel's stock, glancing at Alinta as she ponderously walked about while busily washing up after dinner. They would have helped but the aboriginal woman had insisted on doing the dishes and feeding the dogs herself.

"Just as independent as a Yank I know," Carmen whispered, loud enough that Fabiola heard her too, and Mel started to laugh at the dig. She'd complained good-naturedly about how Alinta was becoming more assertive as she learned English.

"She has learned to speak her mind when she knows the words," she bragged, proud of the woman and her prowess in the language.

Carmen smiled for her friend, realizing that she had fallen in love with the pregnant woman. Fabiola was surprised to see that too. She hadn't thought about it before, and now, realizing that Mel was a woman and not the man she had originally thought her to be, she realized the unusual relationship that might ensue. It gave her food for thought.

Carmen and Fabiola only stayed two days, helping to finish building the fold and listening to Mel's plans. Mel sent them on their way along with a couple letters she had written that were to be mailed as soon as anyone came to the station with supplies or left to go back to civilization with the station mail. She had told them she intended to buy more sheep, cattle, and horses. She also stated she would be hiring a couple of stockmen, but she insisted that would not happen until next year or maybe the year after next, as she still wanted her peace and quiet.

Mel waved as they left, seeing the empty packsaddles on the extra horses. The two women and a couple vaqueros who knew her returned the wave. The stockman nodded, wondering at the odd man, who preferred to be all alone in the far Outback with his woman and large flock. They hadn't been privy to the conversations between the women, knowing their place was not with the station owners.

CHAPTER TWELVE

Mel was loving the freedom of exploring this land and wished she could go on forever. Realistically, she realized she would have to settle down somewhere soon. It was getting too hard to get Alinta on a horse, and she thought it might become too dangerous for the pregnant woman to ride, no matter how slowly or carefully they rode. She was getting nervous at the direct looks the woman was giving her, worried that she was projecting thoughts or feelings onto the woman that weren't her own.

They were heading out to build their sixth fold when she stumbled across a beautiful valley that was hidden among the hills and dips of land that encompassed what she hoped would eventually become her station. She found the hidden valley while searching for some of her sheep that had broken out of the fold. She didn't know if it was because they were due to give birth soon or were just flighty like some sheep, but while using the dogs to find them, she came across a path she knew was not man-made and followed it. Her horse stepped carefully, and as they crested a hill, which gave her a beautiful view of the Outback, she happened to look over the edge, and her breath caught at the sight before her. The green valley held not only her missing sheep, but kangaroos, wallabies, and other animals she didn't recognize. A small waterfall fell from the rocks on one side, and a stream meandered through the valley, becoming lost on the far side. She realized this might be the very spot she wanted for her home paddock. The valley itself was hidden by the countless hills that led up to it, and this could be her backyard, secure and for her own uses only. The beauty of it alone was something she wanted to capture and call her own. It was to the east and slightly south of the fifth fold they had built. They decided they had gone far enough north and were now swinging back.

"Find him sheep?" Alinta asked as she walked laboriously up the hill behind Mel, using her stick to help herself.

"Alinta, you shouldn't be walking out here," Mel told her, worrying that she was doing too much again and the walking would be bad for the baby that seemed to be jutting out of her. She'd seen an arm move across the pregnant woman's stomach last week, and it looked painful.

"Baby strong," she told her, smiling at the other woman's concern. Her adoration for Mel shone in her eyes, but she couldn't seem to make Mel see that she wanted more. She didn't know how, and she certainly didn't have the words she needed to tell the large woman.

Mel got off her horse and held out her hand to the aboriginal woman, and when she was standing next to her, she said, "Look at

that," pointing to the hidden valley with sheep grazing in it along with kangaroos and wallabies.

"Ohhh," Alinta breathed out, appreciating how beautiful the land was. She'd seen more of the Outback than any of her people, she was sure of it. She was so grateful to have someone to share it with, and soon, she would have a child. She rubbed her stomach and felt a well-aimed kick. She smiled as she looked up at Mel, hoping she would want to raise the child with her. Strangely, she wished that Mel was the father but understood that wasn't possible. Still, she hoped for so many things and wished she had the words to express herself.

"I think this is where I'll build our home paddock," Mel explained.

"Home?" Alinta asked, unsure of the word.

"Yes, where we will live permanently, but we will have other paddocks for stockmen to take our sheep, like they do at Twin Station." Mel knew she wasn't explaining it adequately, but she wasn't always sure how much Alinta understood or what words she remembered. Her phenomenal memory made Mel feel ashamed whenever she caught herself talking pidgin English to the woman. The intelligent woman unintentionally reminded Mel to always treat her as an equal. Just because she didn't have the education Mel had didn't mean she didn't know a lot. In fact, she had taught Mel a lot since she had met her. She wished she could have more with Alinta but didn't want to take advantage of the pregnant, young woman. The last time she had been involved with a young woman…she squashed all thoughts of Abigail Baxter, now Worthington. She had released her memories of Abigail on the long ship ride out here. Those were better left in the past.

"You build fold, hut?" she asked.

"Yes, we will build a fold there," she pointed to a spot out of the way of the path that led into the valley. She began squinting as she imagined the house she wanted. The view from the porches would look out into this green, beautiful spot. The sheds and barns she intended to have would be down to the right of the house and out of the way, in no way impeding the view. "We will build sheds, barns, and corrals over there," she pointed to another spot as she got excited. "For now, I'll get the sheep," she brought herself back to Earth, knowing she could get excited by her many plans. She sent the dogs down the animal trail after the sheep, who looked up from their grazing as they spotted them. The dogs soon rounded up the sheep and brought them back up the path. Mel sent them back towards the temporary fold they had broken out of.

Mel walked with Alinta back to their camp, not willing to get back on the horse she now led. Mel enjoyed walking with this woman and wished desperately she could make her feelings known. She worried that she would be rejected, or the woman would be appalled at the suggestion of two women being together. Then, there was the way that Alinta acquiesced to almost everything Mel wanted to do, a product of her upbringing, or so Mel thought. If she gave into everything, would she feel compelled if Mel asked her to be her partner? Would she even understand what Mel was asking?

They started to build the fold the next day, using the sheep to mow the grasses around the site Mel had chosen. This one would be much larger than any of the others she had built. They were almost done with it a couple weeks later when the sheep began to give birth. Mel had known it would be hard being the only one with so many sheep giving

birth at the same time. Alinta tried to help, but she was limited by her girth, and Mel didn't allow her to do much.

"Please, just keep me supplied with hot stew and keep me warm," Mel asked when Alinta waddled out to the never-ending flock of sheep that were giving birth. Mel was becoming exhausted as she went from sheep to sheep that needed assistance. Fortunately, most of the sheep gave birth without help. She had learned over a year ago on Foster's station that there was a difference between a sheep bleating in distress and bleating for no reason; the tones were quite different. Alinta learned to recognize the difference too, and several times, she brought a distressed sheep to Mel's attention, wanting to help her. Alita didn't quite understand Mel's concern for her welfare. No one had ever been concerned like that for her before. As she began to recognize the concern, she couldn't fathom it at first, and then, she was hopeful. She helped where Mel would allow her, making her aware of some of the sheep that needed help, but there were so many. For the most part, the sheep gave birth with no noise, a natural defense against predators and their own vulnerabilities.

The days began to blend as Mel wearily went about her job. The dogs kept a diligent watch, but two of them were nearing their own time and were becoming limited in their abilities. The smell of the afterbirths attracted predators, not just dingoes but also hawks, other birds, and animals that were drawn by the odors. The dogs were busy keeping them away. Mel took catnaps for days, stumbling awake as she heard another sheep giving birth. Herding them slowly back to the nearly finished fold gave her time to catch a meal and maybe a bit of sleep before she was up once again to tend to her large flock. She kept her musket nearby to fire at any dingoes she saw, cursing herself for not having sought them out and hunted them before. She'd known the time was near for the sheep and should have eliminated the threat. Her lack of sleep nearly cost her several lambs when the dingoes attacked. She fired at them, first with one barrel and then another, and the dogs converged on the predators and fought them. Frightened at seeing the two pregnant bitches among the throng, Mel pulled at the dogs, earning a snap and a bite from them. Blood was streaming down her hand where she was bitten, but she got the bitches away and tied up while the rest of the dogs chased away the dingoes. She tied the two bitches up near their hut as Alinta looked on wide-eyed. She quickly helped to bandage Mel's hand as Mel reloaded her gun.

Mel went back to work as soon as she could, realizing she wouldn't save them all. She skinned the carcasses of the sheep and lambs they lost, putting them into bags and cutting up the meat and drying it out with the intention of using it for dog food. She wouldn't eat the dried mutton, but with water added, the dogs might. Alinta helped with that, proudly using the knife she so admired to cut up the carcasses once Mel explained what she wanted done with them. Mel knew that some grazers would have burned the carcasses, but she didn't want to waste anything, and the dried meat could be stored in the extra empty kegs she had from supplies or even in the bags that went on the packhorses. Rows of drying meat hung around the fire, the smoke keeping flies at bay as Mel continued to help her sheep.

It wasn't until she let the entire flock out into the hidden valley that she realized how many of the three- and four-year-old sheep had given birth to twins and triplets. There were even a few quadruplets. They had more than doubled the size of her flock. Some had rejected the extras, which she had seen on Foster's station, and she attempted some

of the tricks, but there were a few that would die, so she slaughtered them, having no intention of watching them starve to death because their mothers would not feed them. These were added to the dried dog food supply, and Alinta willingly cut them up for her.

Mel cried from exhaustion, startling Alinta, who had never seen the larger woman cry before. Alinta held Mel tenderly, her arms conveying the deep empathy she was unable to express in words yet. Mel slept in the Aborigine's arms that night as the births tapered off and exhaustion took her over. She woke up frantic, afraid she had missed some of the sheep, and was surprised to find Alinta holding her. The woman smiled down at Mel, caressing the side of her face as the Yank looked up into her face, startled. Mel leaned up and placed her lips on the other woman's, surprising the other woman, who touched her lips wonderingly with her fingertips at the touch that seemed to tingle. Mel smiled, pulling away and getting up to check on her sheep.

"It looks like a good crop," she said as she gazed at the many sheep with their lambs gamboling along beside them. Some were still too wobbly to do much more than fall flat on their faces as she let them out to graze. Slowly, the dogs pushed them into the valley, pushing aside the native wildlife as the sheep spread out to munch on the grasses, and their lambs learned to walk and eventually run, getting stronger with every day.

Mel was pleased she hadn't lost too many sheep during this busy time, but she knew she wouldn't want another season like this. Looking at the many sheep from her vantage point above them, she realized there were well over ten thousand sheep in that valley, and if every one of the lambs grew up, she'd have a flock too vast for her and her dogs to handle alone. She glanced at Alinta, who smiled at her shyly, still in wonder over their shared kiss that morning. She brought Mel a plate as she watched over her sheep and stayed to watch her eat the food she had prepared for her.

Mel started to castrate and mulse the lambs, throwing the tissue into a bucket until it was full and then dumping it onto the fire where she burned it. The smell was delicious except for the burnt wool, but she didn't want to leave the skin around where the smell of tissue would attract predators. Some of the birds were almost as bad as the dingoes, and she wasn't so sure they couldn't carry off the lambs. Now, she worried about moving the sheep to one of her other folds as well as the ones she had planned to build. The other folds weren't big enough for a flock of this size, although the lambs were still small. She couldn't stay here at what would become their home paddock indefinitely. The bitches were due to give birth soon, and not long after that, Alinta was due, at least, she thought that was true.

Mel finally decided to head for one of the paddocks, going so slow that she worried more about the sheep and their lambs being in the greatly enlarged rope fold and got very little sleep as she guarded them. The two pregnant dogs and Alinta were on the extra horses, the packs so low that she tied the two dogs on the top and Alinta sat on her sidesaddle looking enormous. Mel was relieved to reach one of the other folds, giving the home paddock time to heal from the many sheep grazing on it. She immediately built another hut for them to live in without Alinta's help as she couldn't get about much anymore.

They were both wrong on the time. Mel had hoped she had another month, but the hut was barely built when Alinta went into labor, giving birth to her daughter almost effortlessly. Mel stared wonderingly at this little miracle, noticing the white features and skin color on the tiny,

perfect girl. She wiped her down with a cloth and handed her to her mother as Alinta lay back against their supplies and looked eagerly at the baby.

Mel burned the afterbirth in the fire and checked on the sheep. She was shocked to discover that one of the bitches had given birth the previous night. She hadn't heard any of it in her desire to help Alinta give birth. The woman was so hearty that she might have done it all alone and knotting and cutting the cord was Mel's only contribution. She had worried that she would have to reach up inside Alinta like she did for the sheep occasionally, but fortunately, that hadn't been necessary. She returned to the hut to watch Alinta offer her breast to the hungry infant. The sucking began immediately, and she saw the woman cringe slightly as the baby latched on to her engorged nipple. That looked painful to Mel, and she turned to go to the fire and stoke it, filling the pot, or billy as it was called, with water and then sprinkling tea in it. She watched the billy until it boiled. It was simply a metal can with a wire handle attached to it. Suspending it over the fire, she waited for the tea to steep and the water to boil before pouring it in a pannikin, a small metal drinking cup. No one seemed to drink coffee in this country, and her supply had long ago run out. She'd learned to drink tea as everyone seemed to enjoy the beverage, but she still missed her coffee. She took some tea to Alinta, who sipped at the hot beverage, too fascinated by her offspring to notice much. Mel woke her to eat a little before letting her go back to sleep when she left to take the sheep out to pasture. She left her with food and drink nearby.

Walking past the bitch, she stopped to watch the pups drinking along the teats while the dog licked and cleaned them. They looked like five fine pups, but she had never seen puppies this young before.

The bitch had chosen a spot near the fold but out of the way where an overhang of the wood sheltered her slightly. It was a smart place for the dog to have chosen. Mel praised her, and the dog's butt wiggled in response as she went back to proudly cleaning her pups. Mel continued to the fold, past where the other bitch was tied up. She was wondering at the miracle of birth as she saddled her horse and then let down the wood bars, the other dogs rising to help her slowly herd the sheep out to graze.

Sitting on a hillside and watching her enormous flock, she had nothing but time to think about what she wanted. That little girl would require two parents. Mel would never have a child of her own body; she had realized that fact long ago. Something about that little girl stirred something inside her. She knew of her attraction to Alinta, but did that extend to her daughter? Did she want to parent Alinta's child with her? Did she want a child of her own? She shook her head as the thoughts swirled all day long. As she took the sheep to water and began to slowly gather them and push them back to the fold, she watched the lambs prancing about, not even aware that not so long ago, they were unsteady on their feet and just newly born. She shook her head at the miracle of life and how many of these fragile creatures would grow up and complete the cycle again. Not her though. She would never have a child of her body, but that didn't bother her too much.

Mel was surprised to see Alinta up and moving about the hut as she passed with the sheep that evening. She waved and was pleased to see a smile of greeting on the woman's face. She found the woman striking, earthy, and even more attractive than she had been before. The wonder of it all surprised her. She quickly removed the saddle

from her horse, wiped it down, and hobbled it with the other horses. She wondered if perhaps, the sheep and horses should be kept separate, especially since the sheep were slowly growing out of the sturdy fold she had built. There were simply too many animals to be kept in there together. Fortunately, more than half of them were still lambs, but that wouldn't be the case when she returned from having them shorn.

As Mel watched the sheep grazing during the day, she also thought about the long trip back to Twin Station to get the sheep shorn. According to her calendar—the stick that she used to count the days— she should be heading south soon to catch the shearers. She realized that barring any catastrophes, next year, the shearers would have to come here to her station, and she wanted to be ready for them. Herding over ten thousand sheep would be a nightmare, and it would make more sense for them to come to her. She would need men on her place, and she wanted to build a house at the home paddock. All of this plagued her mind, and as she glanced over where Alinta moved with the baby in a cloth she had slung around her neck, she thought about all her responsibilities. Everything was weighing heavily on her broad shoulders.

"Have you decided on a name for your daughter?" she asked Alinta, wondering how much she understood her English words after their many months together.

Alinta was surprised. She had never thought to name her own child. In her tribe it was the man's right to name his children. She looked at Mel in consternation. "No," she admitted, almost ashamed to admit it. "Mel name daughter?"

"You want me to name your daughter?" she asked to clarify, something she had gotten into the habit of doing long ago because it helped Alinta with her English.

Alinta nodded, understanding clearly what she was asking.

"I'll think about it. A name is very important." Mel considered, sucking on her pipe and looking at the child, who was held in its mother's arms as she moved about busily, putting together their dinner and getting the dogs' food ready at the same time. She hadn't needed much time to rest after giving birth. What an amazing woman! Remembering her tutor's Greek philosophy courses, she thought of the Amazon women, one of which was incarnate standing before her. Primitive perhaps but just as strong as those warrior women of old.

Alinta nodded again, pleased that Mel would name her child. She looked down at the little girl, amazed that she had given birth to her. Her skin was much lighter than Alinta's own, and while she didn't understand all that genetics had given the girl or really know who her father was, she knew that somehow the white man had influenced her daughter's makeup. She didn't quite fully grasp that the rape of her person had caused this little girl, that Bradley's use of her body had impregnated her. Instead, she thought of the first time she had felt the little girl move inside her and how much Mel had influenced her. She thought of Mel as the baby's other parent. She felt Mel's influence, her presence in Alinta's life, caused the baby not only to be female but to look white.

As Alinta finished feeding the dogs and moved to dish up their own food, Mel thought about the name. As she ate, she explained her reasoning to Alinta, not knowing how much the woman might understand.

"There was an ancient woman in Greece, an Amazon woman, who was the enemy of a great god named Achilles," she told the woman, who listened, unmoving, as she stared raptly at Mel. Mel took a bite of her food, gesturing with her fork as she spoke. "That woman fought with a queen named Penthesilea against the god Achilles at a place called Troy." She really wondered how much of this story Alinta would comprehend since she didn't have the same understanding about other places, but somehow, she was determined to make her understand. "The name Ainia," she pronounced it ah-nee-aa, "means swiftness." Alinta was probably the fastest woman Mel had ever seen before her pregnancy slowed her down. "Your daughter will be named for an Amazon woman, and her name will mean swiftness." She finished her meal and put down the plate, holding out her hands for the baby that Alinta handed her. "Let's name your daughter, Ainia, which sounds like your name Alinta, but it is even more special for she is named after that amazing Amazon woman." She looked down at the little girl, seeing that Alinta had cleaned her up completely since the morning when she had given birth. She smiled at the little girl and asked, "Are you, Ainia?"

Alinta didn't understand everything Mel told her, but she did understand that she was naming her daughter after another tribe woman, an Amazon. She was happy that the name was like hers, and she understood that her daughter's name meant swiftness. She would ask Mel to repeat the story of the fight between the queen and the god and Ainia's involvement in it many times. It would become her favorite story, and she felt Mel had chosen correctly, as she had known she would. The white woman knew so many things and didn't mind sharing them with Alinta. She was pleased with the name Mel had given her daughter.

CHAPTER THIRTEEN

Mel thought the trip to the Twin Station with all their sheep, lambs, horses, dogs (one with pups), and a woman with a new baby was all a bit much. The lambs were rambunctious, running around their dams, then running ahead and playing with each other. Then suddenly, they would realize they were alone, the dogs were scary, and they needed to find their mamas. Their bleats were constant and seemingly endless. Over six thousand lambs were calling to their patient mamas, all behaving the same way. The dogs were being worked hard and were exhausted daily as Mel stretched the fold, praying that nothing would frighten the overly large flock. She had expected twins to double her flock, but there were enough triplets and quads that she was almost frightened by her good luck, and she worried constantly that something bad would happen.

Strapped to the horse Alinta was riding was a bag containing the pups that the bitch wouldn't allow out of her sight. The dog followed the horse constantly, eagerly waiting for the time when they would stop, so the puppies could be let down, and she could nurse them and clean them in her anxiety over their welfare. Alinta wore a wrap that kept Ainia strapped tightly to her, so she could easily breastfeed the infant as she rode when it became necessary. Behind Alinta were the horses with all the gear piled on them, including poles for making the temporary folds that were dragged behind them.

Mel found the only time she got a proper night's sleep on the trip was when she approached a permanent fold and was able to put the flock inside, but even that was becoming harder as the lambs were growing at a phenomenal rate, making it impossible for a flock this size to fit in what Mel and Alinta had built. In the middle of the drive, the other bitch gave birth. She lost two of her puppies before Mel could help her remove the one overly large pup that had stuck in her birth canal. They were two days at this fold, the massive flock mowing down the grasses at an alarming rate. The dirt that the flock kicked up created a dust storm, and no one wanted to ride the drag, including the dogs whose job it was to follow behind. Still, they did their best, and Mel secured a second pack for the surviving pups, which was followed by the bitch. Having both dogs out of commission hindered the amount of work that could be done with the large flock. It slowed them down further, and Mel already felt like they were moving at a snail's pace.

The constant worry about dingoes, keeping the flock intact, and making sure that the puppies, the bitches, Alinta and the baby were all taken care of wore on Mel and caused her to lose weight as she worked

extra hard to make sure she wasn't failing any of them. She was becoming short-tempered from lack of sleep, the fatigue was making the work much harder, and the length of the trip was wearing on her soul.

As they left the last permanent fold and headed onto Twin Station, Mel noticed a dust cloud approaching from afar. She spotted it from the top of one of the hills they climbed. The rolling hills before her gave no sign of other sheep, and the dust cloud wasn't large enough for a flock, so she wondered what was kicking up the dust. She found out hours later when Carmen and Fabiola came riding out of the trees with five packhorses behind them and only two vaqueros to protect the senora.

"We thought something had happened to you. It's late!" Carmen explained as she took in the enormous flock. "I see you've been busy."

"More than I could have ever dreamed," Mel answered, relieved to see her friends. The vaqueros nodded and immediately handed off the packhorses to Alinta before heading out to help keep the flock in line.

"You didn't lose any sheep?" Fabiola asked, surprised.

"Oh, yes. We lost plenty of sleep, but it's these guys that really made it worthwhile," she teased, indicating the baby, the puppies visible from the sacks on both sides of Alinta's saddle, and the anxious bitches following at her horse's feet.

"Oh, your *baby*," Carmen's voice changed, sounding like she was crooning as she spoke to Alinta. "What did you have? What did you name it?"

"Baby is girl, and Mel named her Ainia after the Greek Amazon. It like my name," Alinta told her proudly.

Carmen and Fabiola looked at a blushing Mel in surprise, and Carmen smiled. "That's lovely," she told the delighted mother. "I'd like to see her when we stop later. Nothing felt as good as holding my babies," she reminisced. "Your English," she exclaimed, "has gotten much better!" she complimented the surprised mother, who smiled shyly.

Mel smiled, enjoying the interaction and relieved to see them. "Have the shearers left?" she worried as she addressed Fabiola.

"No," the Australian shook her head. "We told them we were waiting on some of our additional flocks and convinced them to stay on. They had a couple of our flocks left to do yet, so we should get this flock to them in time. That one was worried about you though," she said, nodding towards a now blushing Carmen.

"You said you'd come in time for the shearers," she accused to hide her embarrassment over her concern for her friend.

"I tried, but this is a lot, and I'll admit we need help."

"There are a couple of men at the station. They say they were answering an ad someone placed for you?" Carmen inquired.

Mel nodded, relieved. She had more ads she wanted to write and would do so in the evenings when they finished the drive. She hoped there was mail for her along with the men who had answered her ad.

They discussed the sheep. Mel was happy to see her friend and her friend's cousin. She was hoping to make Fabiola a friend too. She felt the potential was there but understood that the woman hadn't known how to take her before. Now, with nearly a year behind her, she must understand there was friendship only between Mel and Fabiola's cousin and nothing more.

"Who are the carters?" she asked innocently, but both Carmen and Alinta knew the question wasn't as innocent as it seemed.

"Oh, the ones I use every year. This will probably be the last year I use them though. Carmen has uncovered some discrepancies in their books and invoices over the years."

"Would the name Bradley be among any of the men working for them?" She glanced in time to see Alinta flinch slightly and then looked at Carmen, who was shaking her head.

"No, I don't recall any of the men being addressed as Bradley. Why? Is there a problem?"

"Well, one of the carters we met on our way out here was named Bradley, and I'll shoot the bugger on sight if he comes anywhere near us again," Mel said in a no-nonsense tone, then dropped the subject.

Fabiola looked startled, exchanging a look with Carmen and then looking back at the big grazer. She glanced at the gun Mel wore on her hip as well as the double-barreled musket in her scabbard, readily at hand. Looking back at Carmen, she happened to see the pleased expression that passed on Alinta's face before she looked down at her baby.

"Well, these sheep aren't going to get to your home paddock any faster without our help," Mel stated, walking her horse off in another direction and halting their friendly conversation.

Carmen and Fabiola exchanged another look before they too went to help with the flock. Alinta glanced at the three women and tightened her hold on the reins of the many packhorses she was now holding. She managed to cuddle Ainia closer as she urged her horse on. Mel had been a good teacher, and Alinta was no longer frightened of the strange beast, realizing she was in control.

That night at the fire, Mel breathed a sigh of relief. Having more help to bring the flock in meant there was less danger of them breaking out of the temporary fold. That night was the first good night's sleep she'd gotten in a long while. She enjoyed it before getting up early to take a turn guarding the animals. She wondered if the dogs could sense her ease as they too seemed more relaxed. She stopped to pet the puppies that Alinta had taken from the bags, so the bitches could cuddle their broods. Both bitches wiggled their butts in greeting, simulating wagging tails that were no longer there. She heard Ainia fussing and Alinta trying to calm her.

"May I take the baby for you?" she offered and held out her large hands.

Alinta didn't hesitate. She had fed the baby, but she wouldn't settle down. She watched as Mel talked softly to the infant as she walked off into the early morning light to do her rounds, knowing just the presence of humans kept some predators away.

Alinta rose to go in the brush and do her morning absolutions. She was using water more often now that she had learned Mel liked things clean. She had observed Mel washing the baby several times. While Alinta would have rubbed sheep fat on the baby, Mel washed it off. She did allow Alinta to rub the baby with crushed leaves that warded off the constant flies and mosquitos, but she used them too. Alinta stoked the fire as the vaqueros sleepily awoke and rose.

"Good morning," Carmen whispered as she came up to the warmth of the fire to help.

"Good morning," Alinta replied, understanding the greeting now from her months with Mel.

"Where is Ainia?" she asked, hoping she could cuddle some more with the infant like she had before they went to sleep the previous night. Fabiola too had held the baby, if somewhat awkwardly. She'd compared it to a newborn lamb, much to the amusement of the other women.

"Mel took her to calm baby," she said inaccurately, almost shyly, as she wasn't used to communicating with anyone but Mel.

Carmen smiled, knowing Mel had been good with her children on the long trek out here. She wondered if the American had wanted children of her own and if that would ever have been a possibility. Well, if what she suspected between the American and the Australian aboriginal woman was true, that baby was as much Mel's as it was Alinta's. She busied herself, helping the woman to prepare breakfast, so they could all get on their way. It was still a long way across Twin Station.

As they approached the home paddock, other riders rode out to help with the large flock, splitting it into different corrals, so the shearers could start in on the sheep.

Mel and Alinta took one of the empty stockmen's houses, surprised to see a modern house being built on one of the hills beyond the home paddock. "What's that?" Mel asked Carmen as they watched the shearers effortlessly guide their clippers along a sheep. A good shearer was worth their weight in gold as they quickly and efficiently sheared the sheep. Very little blood was spilled, and the maximum amount of wool was taken from the poor beast, who accepted its lot without any fanfare while waiting patiently to be released. Only occasionally did a sheep fight back, and these feisty ones made it interesting for those helping to keep the sheep processed—from pushing them into the chute to pushing them back out into the corrals. Many of them had to seek out their lambs, who had been bleating pitifully while waiting impatiently for their dams, who had been separated from them. It still amazed the women, and even some of the men, how quickly a sheep could find its lamb among all those that were crying out for their mamas.

"Oh, Carmen didn't like our accommodations," Fabiola said as she came up, hearing Mel asking about the building going on at the hillside. She sounded almost British in her tones; the Australian accent nearly eliminated as she informed the American with a twinkle in her eye as she looked at Carmen.

Other men had come all the way from Sydney to do the work Carmen had sent for, riding with the carters, who brought their yearly supplies and planned on staying for months to do the work she had contracted them for. The tone of Fabiola's voice didn't tell Mel whether she was pleased with the building or not.

"I'm going to have to get some buildings on my place as well," Mel admitted. "Maybe I should talk to them about coming where I want my home built when they're done." She'd told them of the hidden valley she had found, describing it in glowing terms.

"They'll be wanting to head back to Sydney when they are done," Fabiola told her, a disparaging note in her voice as she said it. "A couple of them already have the willies from being out here." She'd learned that phrase from Carmen and enjoyed using it.

Carmen and Mel exchanged a look. Both understood that feeling. Several of the men on the way out here had experienced that phenomenon but fortunately, neither of the women had. Both had instead embraced the endless lands and the feel of forever in the Outback. Mel had even commented once that leaving her old life behind hadn't been a problem. Instead, she felt that she had been born for this. *Perhaps, I was bred for this,* she thought as she helped to herd her flock onto the vast Outback.

Fabiola introduced the men, who had come to speak to Mel in answer to her ads. Several of them agreed to hire on for a year, possibly more, as she assessed how they worked with the sheep. She also had a stack of mail that had come with the supplies she ordered.

She discussed the men helping her build a track on her station, so the carts that carried supplies could be hauled in. She explained what she had already built, what she intended to build, and all her other plans. If any wanted to back out at the amount of work she had in the planning, they would have the opportunity now. None did, wanting the jobs because Mel promised an honest day's wage for an honest day's work.

Mel stopped by the chow house to share in the drinking going on there, being personable with the stockmen who were in. She had met a couple of them the last time she was there. Many already had their sheep sheared and were gone, but the few sticking about might be needing a job, if Fabiola and Carmen hadn't already hired them. The two women had warned her away from a couple of the hangers-on as possible troublemakers, and one had already been ordered off the station for making trouble down in the Aborigine's village by pestering the women. Another had angered Mel when he kept eyeing Alinta, especially when she was breastfeeding Ainia. Not wanting to make a scene or restrict Alinta in any way, Mel had simply glared at the man, her mere size intimidating him.

"Mr. Lawrence?" an unfamiliar voice addressed Mel. Not used to being addressed this way, she turned in surprise to see a cleric standing there with his bible in hand. His starch white collar stood out in contrast to his black robes, and he looked at her benevolently. She glanced beyond him to see Carmen looking amused, and Fabiola's eyes danced in amusement.

"Yes?" she asked, wondering if this was a Catholic priest and how she should address him. There was a hint of something in his accent, not Australian and probably not English either.

"I was wondering what you were planning on doing about the welfare of the child?" he asked, as though he were giving her a blessing of some kind.

Mel frowned, not understanding. "What child?" she asked, sounding stupid.

"Why the child of your…wife?" he asked, sounding surprised that she didn't know what he was talking about.

Mel chuckled. "I don't have a wife," she said before she could catch herself, and she saw Carmen and Fabiola both turn away in mirth. Then, she realized what the man of the cloth must be thinking—that Alinta was her common-law wife, and Ainia was her child. Now, he must be thinking the baby was born out of wedlock.

"But the child must be saved! It must be baptized!" he protested. "We must not take advantage of these poor savages, who inhabit this land. Their simple minds must be protected and saved." He held up his bible to emphasize saving the masses.

Mel was amused. She had attended many churches over the years, and she believed in a higher being, but organized religion was not for her, especially not out here. Saving the aboriginal people, indeed. "Have you ever seen these people in action?" she asked him instead, confusing him. "They are one with the lands here. They don't take anything more than they need from the Earth, and they don't need saving." She realized that last line should not have been added. The man objected immediately and began going on about their poor, lost souls. He blathered on for so long that Mel found herself agreeing to have Ainia baptized.

"How in the world did that happen?" she asked Carmen and Fabiola as they walked along, Fabiola yelling at the loitering men to get back to work.

"He wears you down. He's almost as bad as the priests back at the missions in California. They are forever saving the *savages*, as they call them."

"Well, I better go explain to Alinta, so he doesn't frighten her. I've also got about a dozen letters to write," she sighed, remembering the pile of letters she had gone through.

"We should be done with your flock tomorrow," Fabiola reminded her, glancing at the men, the sheep they were shearing, and the many carts the men were filling with wool.

"Oh, that means they will be going soon," Carmen said, obviously enjoying their visit and not wishing for it to end.

"Well, I also have a station to establish," Mel reminded her friend fondly. She'd been thinking of nothing else since they got here, and she was watching Fabiola's setup. Already, Carmen's influence was obvious in the operations of this station and not just in the building of the house on the side of the hill. Carmen had explained that it was out of the path of the creek that had flooded during the rains, and the hill should protect it from the worst of the winds. She also loved its view. Mel thought about her own view and headed to get her horse instead of dealing with her stacks of mail.

"Who is the foreman here?" she asked as she rode up to the house site where six men were industriously working to build a sizeable house. The foundation would be stone. She could see two of the men were making what looked like a mud mix to lay between the native stones.

"I am," a short, bandy-legged man with an Irish brogue told her, sounding defensive.

Mel got down from her horse and held the reins in one hand as she held out her other hand. "I'm Mel Lawrence. I have a station I'm starting up there," her chin pointed vaguely north, not realizing the miles that separated it from this station.

The man shook the proffered hand, eyeing up the large man before him, unaware he was speaking with a woman with powerful shoulders. Building her own folds and handling the axe had increased her muscles, and after wearing men's clothing for years, she was comfortable with everyone assuming she was a man.

"Was that your flocks coming in yesterday?" the man asked.

"Yes, that was my flock," she corrected gently.

"One flock?" he asked, incredulous. He'd seen the size of it.

"Yes, my men were here, and we'll be splitting it up into smaller flocks now." She wasn't about to explain that she had managed the original four thousand on her own and the rest were from this year's crop of lambs. Most years, from what she had learned, they would be

lucky if they got a one-third increase or maybe double. That was why she had chosen three- and four-year-olds, they usually had more offspring and were mature enough to raise them successfully. Carmen and Fabiola had reported that the Merinos they merged with the various flocks were doing well. A few had fallen to dingoes, disease, and other natural disasters, but the majority were doing well. "I was wondering if you and your men would like another commission?" she asked, watching the men working industriously. She was here about his work not her flocks.

"Another commission?" he asked, not sure about the word.

"More work. I need a house, barns, and sheds built on my station," she explained.

The man, Shamus O'Grady, was indeed Irish, and he discussed her needs with her. He advised he would have to send to Sydney for some of the things she wanted. Her job was quite different from the single level ranch house or hacienda-style house without stucco that the senora had asked him to build. "What you're planning is much grander," he said, rolling his Rs and sounding rich.

Mel agreed it was grander and wondered how many of these men would want to stay in the Outback to do the work. She well knew it wasn't for everyone. Some men went crazy when faced with the vast spaces. Carmen had said one of her vaqueros was eventually affected and had to stay in the home paddock instead of tending her horses or the sheep, but they dealt with it and accommodated him because they were all family to her.

"I won't be able to start until I finish working for the senora, you understand?"

Mel nodded, and they squatted in the dust as she drew out what she wanted. "I can put this on paper, but my skills at drawing are limited, and I'm no architect," she admitted.

"I won't be needing no architect," he told her, sounding almost proud of that fact, "but mind you, the fixtures you are wanting will take months to come from the city."

Mel nodded, agreeing with him as they discussed her requirements. She wanted some modern features and wasn't sure if the builder could manage it, but after talking with him for a while, she was certain he could handle the job. As he had said, it would be months before he was done here because the senora also wanted some barns and other things built after the house.

"I'll have my men begin to stack up logs and rocks for you to use when you get there," Mel nodded towards the two men, who were expertly building the wall. "I'll send for some of these things," she indicated the windows and other things she would need for her house and barns.

"You'll have to build a track as well," he teased, having heard of this man from others on the station as they built this house.

"That and another," she agreed, wondering if she would find enough men. She didn't have the sheep to justify more men working for her, but at the same time, if the letters in her stack were any indication, she would know soon if the animals she wished to place on her claimed land would be available, and if they were, then she'd need the men. Either way, she could afford it.

She left him to return to the home paddock, looking down on it from the hill and admiring the view. It was a nice view, the dust rising from the milling sheep hanging over the buildings. She understood why

Carmen was building here. She could tell Fabiola didn't seem to like the idea, and she wondered where Harold was as she hadn't seen him yet.

She returned to the stockmen's house to find Alinta upset. Evidently, the cleric had been there and tried to explain to her how the ceremony of baptism would go, and it upset her. Mel spent a good half hour explaining to the woman that it was for religious purposes, not to drown Ainia. "I would never hurt your daughter," she told the woman time and again as she attempted to calm her. "This is so she can enter the kingdom of God," Mel parroted something she had been taught long ago.

"Kingdom?" Alinta asked, confused.

"Remember when we named Ainia?"

The woman nodded, hoping to understand all the words that Mel told her. That other man had used many words she didn't know.

"I told you of the Greek gods and how Ainia is an Amazon name?"

Alinta nodded and said, "An enemy of Achilles?

"Yes," she answered, pleased with Alinta's memory. "This is about God, the Christian God, and while it won't hurt Ainia, it might help her someday." She was thinking about Ainia growing up and how it would be easier to get along in this English society if she was baptized, even if they were in the Outback and away from most of the masses. Still, one never knew what the future held and how things might change.

"Man say we should marry too," Alinta mentioned. "What be marry?"

Mel suddenly felt very uncomfortable, wondering how to explain that concept. "It's a ceremony where we would pledge ourselves to each other," she said, watching the woman to see if she understood. "It

would mean you would be my mate for all time and I would be yours."
She wondered if she was being too simplistic since it meant a lot more
than that to some people.

"Mean Mel no go away ever? Alinta stay always?"

"Do you want to go away? Do you want to find your family?" she
asked, looking at her, worried. She had thought they were long past the
worry that the woman would go with the Aborigines she had seen, and
she showed no interest in the ones that lived here on the station or the
few they had seen in their own wanderings.

Alinta made a signal with her hand. Mel saw it and knew it meant
no. It had taken her a while to learn these signs from the woman, but
she watched her body language a lot more now than she had when she
first met the woman. "Family no want Alinta now. Mel and Ainia
family now."

"Do you want to marry me?" she asked. "Do you want to make it
permanent and 'right' in the eyes of the white men?" Her heart was
beating frantically right now. She had never considered that she might
marry a woman, not even this woman. Men, yes. A long time ago, she
had thought about marrying, even dreamed about it, but she had
accepted her fate when she realized she was attracted to women and
men didn't want her anyway. She looked into the nearly black eyes of
the striking aboriginal woman, hoping she would say yes, yet fearing
she would say yes.

"You want marry Alinta? Become my mate for all time?" Alinta
too was nervous. She had no plans for ever leaving Mel, but if she
wanted this ceremony, to make it *right* in the eyes of white men as she
said, then Alinta wanted it too.

"Only if you do," she said, but she suddenly felt shy and unsure. "Do you understand that if they knew what I am..." she began, uncertain. She knew they would never marry her to the woman if they knew that she was female.

"That you are grazer?" Alinta asked, stressing the Z in a funny way that Mel found endearing.

Mel smiled as she shook her head and addressed the issue she knew Alinta had figured out long ago. Quietly, almost as though someone else was listening, she said, "No, in the white man's world, they do not let women marry other women."

"Why not?" she asked.

Mel shrugged, not willing to debate it with her now. Her heartbeat felt like it was going to choke her. "That is their way. They do not see the obvious. They do not see that I am not a man, but they see you as a woman." She looked at the physically fit woman. She was solid and beautiful to Mel. "They think marriage is only between a man and a woman. Do you want a man? A real man?"

Alinta was already shaking her head, knowing Mel didn't always see her hand when she made the sign. "I want Mel," she said simply.

Mel was shaking. "Do you want...?" she was afraid to ask the question. They hadn't gone there but that one time. She was amazed when Alinta made her own wishes known.

"Mel, will you do that lip on lip again?"

Mel turned her head slightly, almost as if she hadn't heard correctly. "You liked that lip on lip?" she parodied and then corrected herself, "It's called kissing."

"Kissing?"

"Yes, when you do it, it is called kissing, but it is called a kiss," she explained, feeling foolish.

"Yes, I like kissing," Alinta admitted, remembering the feeling of closeness and the tingles it had engendered.

"Do you want me to kiss you?" Mel asked, her voice getting huskier as she looked intently at Alinta.

The woman nodded, suddenly feeling shy and not knowing why.

Mel took a hesitant step forward and leaned down to the woman. She desired her so but had been afraid to take it any further. It hadn't occurred to her that Alinta might want her in return. Gently, she kissed the woman, her lips feeling wonderful beneath Mel's. At first, Alinta just accepted the kiss, but as Mel continued it, softly opening her own lips, the woman imitated her, and Mel deepened the kiss. Alinta was enjoying the kiss as her hands crept around Mel, feeling the muscles she had so admired on the fit woman.

Alinta was amazed that a meeting of the mouths could feel so good. Her mother hadn't told her about that when she told her to accept a man's touch. She had never said anything about accepting a woman's touch, but to Alinta, Mel was much more than a woman. She was everything to the aboriginal woman…She was Mel. For Alinta, that was everything, and she eagerly accepted Mel's kisses, realizing as time went on that she wanted more and imitating the taller woman, learning. She also realized she wanted Mel's touch and hesitantly put her own arms around the large woman, feeling the broad shoulders as she clasped her to her own body that was becoming warm.

When Mel reluctantly pulled back because her breathing had increased, and she could feel herself becoming very aroused, she stared in Alinta's endless, black eyes and felt like she was falling into them.

They were so dark, so mysterious, and so lovely. She couldn't help comparing them to the night skies she saw here in Australia. She hadn't known years of wanderings had been leading her to this amazing woman. She hadn't believed that *any* woman would want to spend the rest of their life with her.

"I like kiss," Alinta said softly, her own breathing coming harder. She wondered if the weather was changing as her body was growing quite warm.

"I do too," Mel admitted, trying to get her equilibrium back. "I think we should wait until the parson marries us to continue this."

"Why?"

"In the white man's world, you only do things like this with your husband or wife, and even then, you only do them after you are married," she explained, wondering at the women she had been with over the years. This type of play was how she had realized she liked the touch of a woman.

"Then we should do this marry thing," Alinta answered simply. "And the water thing too? For Ainia?" She could hear the baby making waking noises from the bed where she had placed her after feeding her. She would have to check on her shortly.

"Alinta, I want to marry you. I want to make love to you too. Are you sure this is what you want? You don't want to spend the rest of your life with a man?"

"No. Alinta no want man. Ever. Man hurt me. Man hurt mother. Man no good."

"Not all men are like that," she said, trying to be fair. Some men were good. Her father had been an excellent example.

"Alinta want no man. Alinta want Mel," she insisted, trying to make herself clear.

Mel smiled brilliantly, leaning down to kiss the woman again. "Mel want Alinta too," she pidgeoned, wanting her so much it hurt.

CHAPTER FOURTEEN

The marriage of Alinta, a woman of aboriginal descent, to Mel (Melissa) Lawrence from America was performed in the open air of the home paddocks where the sheep were shorn, and the men were packing the bags onto carts to transport them to Sydney. Those in attendance were pleased to witness the event. Very few realized the importance of the event or the true sex of the participants.

"Do you, Mel Lawrence..." the cleric droned, having asked for a middle name that Mel did not supply, "take Alinta..." he hesitated over the fact that this woman had no middle or last name. Alinta had given him the name of her tribe, but he couldn't pronounce it, so in his arrogant, white, male way, he simply ignored it. He had gotten what he wanted with the marriage of these two sinners. It was obvious they had been fornicating since the results of their sins was the child the woman was holding in her arms. He had no idea the baby was not Mel's biological child, and he had no idea that she was also a woman. Only four people in attendance knew Mel's sex, and they weren't telling. "...to be your lawfully wedded wife? To have and to hold from this day forward? For better, for worse, for richer, for poorer, in sickness and in health? To love, cherish, and honor above all others till death do you part, according to God's holy law?"

"I do," Mel said clearly, her throat closing off as the importance of the words penetrated. She was holding Alinta's hands firmly, looking down at the woman earnestly. They were both dressed nicely. Mel had pulled out one of her suits, which was now tighter in the shoulders and looser around the middle. She had given Alinta her only dress, which she pinned in for the occasion. It swam on the shorter woman but looked like a summery gown.

"Do you, Alinta, take Mel Lawrence to be your lawfully wedded husband? To have and to hold from this day forward? For better, for worse, for richer, for poorer, in sickness and in health? To love, cherish, and obey, till death do you part, according to God's holy law?"

Alinta had been ready to say yes. She had been nodding after each thing the man said. She had understood all the words, but he hadn't stopped talking, he kept adding words. Only the fact that Mel had agreed to almost all the same words had her answering in a small voice, "Yes."

"You are supposed to say, I do," he told her condescendingly. He didn't see Mel stiffen at the tone in his voice but Alinta did, and she quickly said, "I do." She didn't know why Mel was suddenly angry. Maybe she was mad at Alinta for not knowing the right way to respond. But Mel was now smiling down on her brilliantly as the man continued

his nonsense words and finally proclaimed that they were, "man and wife." Finally, he gave his permission for Mel to kiss her. Alinta blushed as the white woman leaned down and gave her a peck on the mouth in front of all the witnesses, many whistling and clapping.

The wedding was immediately followed by the baptism of Ainia, who was given a second name and then a third.

"I baptize thee, Ainia Mary Lawrence," the clergyman said, pleased that he could perform this small ceremony for them. He had blessed the water, so it was holy, and he poured it on the child's head, expecting her to cry. Instead, to the amazement of those watching, the child giggled. Mel laughed, and Alinta smiled, but the clergyman was horrified. He had never heard of such a thing. The crying was supposed to signify the bad spirits and the devil leaving a purified child's body. Instead, this child had laughed. He stared in horror at this child of mixed races.

As Mel and Alinta turned away to accept congratulations from those attending, Alinta was surprised to be embraced by the women and kissed on the lips by the men. She didn't like that and would have bolted but for Mel's hand firmly holding her hand and Ainia held in her arms.

Mel saw the Aborigines from the small village watching, some knowingly, and she nodded towards them respectfully, especially the elders, who returned her nod of respect. She had spoken to a few of them who spoke English previously, and she had told them they would be welcome at her station too, if they so desired. She would need workers, and if they knew of others, they should come see the station she was going to build.

Mel couldn't believe how much the documents filled out by the clergyman meant to her. Seeing her name on the marriage certificate meant as much to her as Ainia's baptismal paper. She rolled them up carefully, tying them with a ribbon and planning to tuck them away with her other important papers.

"Well, you did it," Carmen said knowingly, leaning up to pull Mel down for a kiss on the cheek. "I hope you will both be very happy."

"I hope we will too. Thank you," she told her friend.

Fabiola wasn't as friendly, but she too wished the large woman happiness. "I'm glad you decided on that land north of us. If I had known about your valley, maybe I would have expanded up there. That will certainly be a huge station, and I'd rather have a friend there." She held out her hand to shake Mel's, and the American took it gladly. She wondered briefly if Ainia would grow up to be as beautiful as this woman of mixed races, and she looked at the woman speculatively, wondering about her as she glanced between Carmen and the station owner.

Harold was next, having returned from helping one of the stockmen get his sheep out to new pasturage and checking some of the southern paddocks they were hoping to reuse. He heartily congratulated Mel but moved on quickly, not acknowledging Alinta, and Mel noted that. He moved determinedly to the table where some of the stockmen's wives had set up some rum in a keg as well as some food for a little celebration. The men packing up the bags of wool rotated out, so they could get a share of the rum and a little food before they departed. The carters were anxious to be on their way knowing it was a long trek back to Sydney.

That evening, Mel handed the lead carter a bag with mail that could be sent out from Wilcannia or Menindee, depending on which direction the man decided to travel. The men were leaving early the next day, and a mail carrier would take it from there, much faster than the carter could. It would take months for him to make his way back to Sydney with his full carts of wool. There was much more than he had anticipated, and he hadn't had a chance to discuss next year's cartage with the station owner. He had no idea that Fabiola and Carmen didn't intend to use his services next year, and some of the mail he carried contained inquiries to other drayage companies for both Twin Station and the newly formed Lawrence Station.

Mel had spent the afternoon after her wedding going through the large pile of mail that had been waiting for her from her lawyer, her accountant, Mrs. Waters, and surprisingly, a letter from Abigail in England. She had written Mel soon after she arrived in Sydney to let her and other people she wanted to stay in contact with know of her new *home* and where to reach her. There were also a few other letters, and she spent the time answering them all and writing quite a few new ones. She wasn't sure how to address her marriage to a woman in her letter to the lawyer here in Australia and thought it best that she think about that for a while before mentioning it. She did, however, make Alinta and Ainia Lawrence her heirs, writing to her father's lawyers, now hers, in America and England. For all they knew, she could have adopted them. It would take time for the letter to reach the Americas and England, so she had some breathing room.

"What is that?" Alinta asked as she nursed Ainia. The dress she had enjoyed was long gone, and she was back in her man's long shirt and miners' pants with her feet bare.

"This is writing," she explained as she finished up one letter, addressed it, and sealed it.

"What is writing?" the inquisitive and always interested woman asked.

Mel realized her wife—how she loved the sound of that word—had never seen her read or write. That gave her another thought. She would write to the lawyer and request some books be sent to her. Thinking about that further, she wanted the classics and perhaps, some basic books would be good to teach her wife how to read and write. Someday, she would also teach her daughter how to read and write. "This is how we communicate across long distances. This is from America, the land where I came from," she said, pointing to the letter she had just answered from her American lawyers. "That one is from England, from a friend of mine that lives there." She had written Abigail too, knowing it might be a year before she heard from her again. Still, ships went to England and the Americas all the time, and it was likely the mail service from Sydney to the interior that would take a lot of time. She'd explained to all involved how far out the station she was establishing was and why it was so long between letters.

"You teach Alinta?"

"Sure, I'll be happy to teach you," she replied, having just had that thought. "We will teach Ainia too someday." She was so happy. She had a companion and a daughter, perhaps, for the rest of her life. She wanted it to be for the rest of her life, but Mel was a realist. They lived so far away from everything and things could happen.

Alinta was happy too. She didn't know what the future held, but with Mel as her mate, she was looking forward to finding out. She looked down at her daughter and held her tighter, knowing they were

safe with this woman-man, and Mel wanted them to be with her forever. She looked down at the odd little ring that Mel had purchased from one of the stockmen, who had lost the woman he was going to marry. She thought it an odd custom to wear such metal, but she also thought it very pretty after she got used to seeing it on her left hand. Mel had explained it went on that finger because white men thought it went directly to their hearts. She explained this with a sweet smile on her face, and Alinta's heart was happy too.

~THE END~

About the Author

K'Anne Meinel is the BEST-SELLING author of LAWYERED, REPRESENTED, SAPPHIC SURFER, DOCTORED, VEIL OF SILENCE, SURVIVORS, VETTED and CAVALCADE as well as several other books including her first, SHIPS which was written in 2003 over the course of two weeks. A gypsy at heart, she has lived in many locations and plans to continue roaming. Videos of several of her books are available on YouTube outlining some of the locations of her books and telling a little bit more…giving the readers insight into her mind as she created these wonderful stories. As of this date she has more than 102 published works including shorts, novellas, and novels. She is an American author born in Milwaukee, Wisconsin and raised in Oconomowoc. Upon early graduation from high school she went to a private college in Milwaukee and then moved to California for seventeen years before returning to the state. Many of her stories have Wisconsin in them as settings for her wonderful, realistic, and detailed backgrounds. Named the lesbian Danielle Steel of her time, K'Anne continues to write interesting stories in a variety of genres in both the lesbian and mainstream fiction categories. Her website is www.kannemeinel.com.

If you have enjoyed **OUTBACK BRED**, I hope you will enjoy this excerpt from
PIONEERING

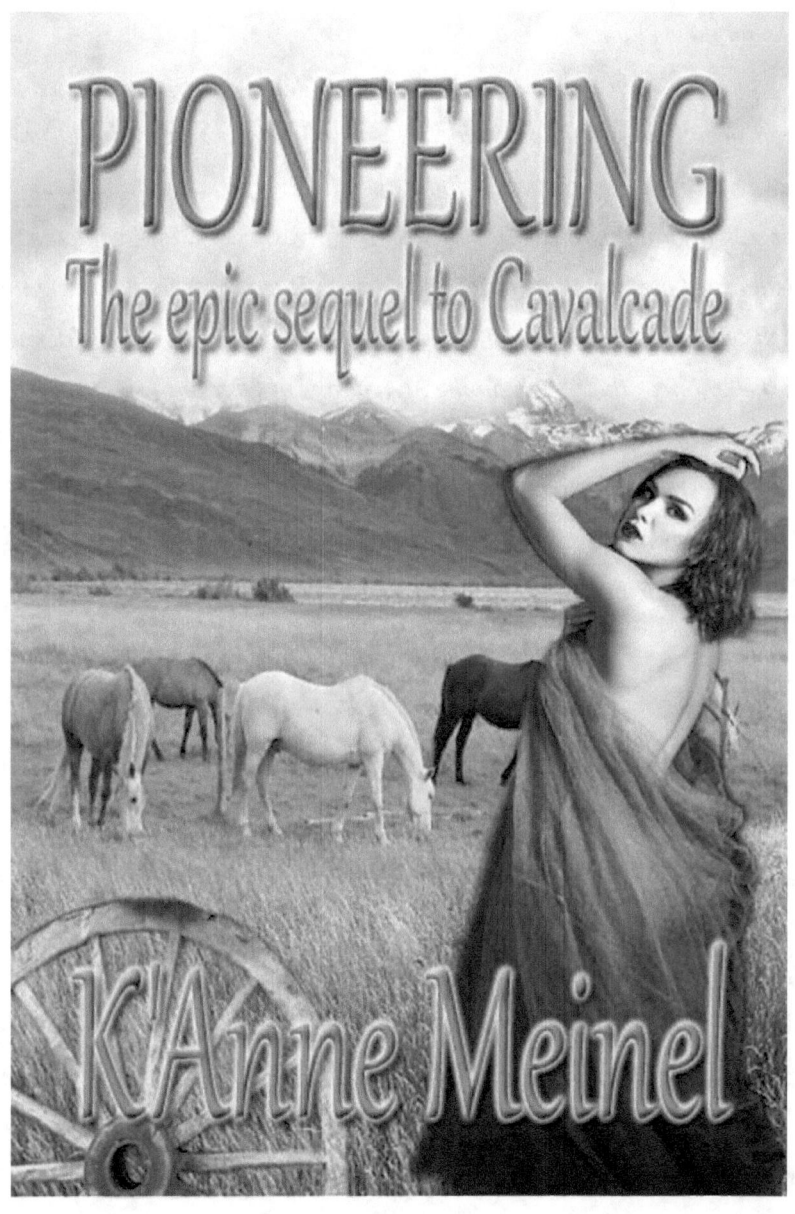

One family's saga had just begun…In the epic sequel to Cavalcade, we learn what happens to the Herriots when they arrive in Oregon and take up their claim.

Erin and Molly arrive in Oregon with their family where they have been granted six hundred and forty acres of land under the Organic Laws of Oregon. They must build their home, farm the land, and eke out a living on this piece of raw land. Wolves, bears, and wildcats are the least of their worries in this new land. Hard work and trusting that each will do their very best are the keys to conquering the wilderness as they pioneer their lives on the high plains of Oregon!

Come along as the Herriot family lives a life few have attempted in this wilderness near the Blue Mountains of Oregon. You won't want to miss Pioneering, the final half of the fantastic pair of prequels to Vetted and Vetted Further!

CHAPTER ONE

"Six hundred acres! Can you *farm* six hundred acres?" Molly marveled when Erin explained.

Erin chuckled and shook her head. She too was amazed at the present they had been given for traveling to Oregon. "Well, maybe not *this* year," she answered modestly, sharing a huge smile with her wife. She waited a moment and said with a note of wonderment in her voice, "Six hundred and forty acres. Who'd a thought?" Why, the farm back in Ohio had been only forty acres and they had fought for it with trees and Indians and rocks. She looked at the land they were heading for, thrilled to realize that all they had to do was work it and improve it to claim it. "We can also raise cattle, horses, and sheep," she reminded her, their seed stock having made the trip with them.

"You already filed?" she asked, sounding slightly hurt.

"I did. I didn't know what I'd find here, and I wanted to claim it for our family before someone else filed on it."

"Is the area settling up?"

"I haven't the faintest idea. We didn't see anyone for days, and it will take us a couple days to get there. But it's ours, Molly, all ours!" she said, putting her arms around the smaller woman and swinging her around and around as she shouted.

"What? What's ours? What's going on?" the children came running. Queenie started barking at the noise.

"Your pa has found our homestead and filed on it," Molly announced, pleased to be the one to tell them.

The children cheered and clapped, happy to hear this news and asking questions a mile a minute.

"Wait, wait, wait. We have to head down to our land tomorrow, and it's going to take at least a couple days to get there."

"Can't we go now?" someone asked.

"Well, we could get in a couple miles," she looked around at Molly, wondering if they should. It was late in the afternoon and she was as anxious as any of them to head down to what was now *their* land.

"No, it's too late in the day, and I don't want to camp by lantern light in a strange area. We will start out tomorrow," Molly vetoed, getting up to put together a dinner for them all.

"Let's move those sheep, so they continue to crop the grass until sunset," Erin encouraged the children, signaling the dogs to move them. She didn't need the children, but unless Molly called one or two to help with dinner, it would keep them out of her hair. Erin scooped up Timmy, lifting him high in the air and hearing his giggles. She was happy, and she wanted to share it with her family.

"What's it like?" Molly asked her as they lay side by side later in the tent, the lantern turned low, so they could see each other as they talked.

"There's trees, excellent farmland, and many acres of grazing land," she answered, sitting up to talk, too excited to sleep yet.

"We'll have to plant first thing," Molly marveled aloud, her arms folded under her head.

"We'll have to build a cabin first thing," Erin corrected, already planning it out in her head.

"Shouldn't we–" began Molly, but Erin, in her excitement, interrupted.

"We probably should do everything, but we have to get these children under a roof and then, the stock."

Molly nodded, agreeing but a little aggrieved that she had been interrupted. She let Erin talk on.

"There is a stream nearby that runs through the valley, so we should be able to dig a well for our farm," she continued. "Some of the upper hills are a little parched and won't be good for anything but grazing, but those fields should give us good crops in the coming years…" she would have gone on and on but noticed Molly's silence. Turning, she tried to peer though the dark at her. "Is something wrong? Don't you want the farm anymore?"

"I would say you are making all the decisions these days."

"You did promise to obey me…" she started to tease, referencing their marriage vows.

Molly sat up slightly, indignant. "I won't obey against my better judgement…" she began angrily and then, realizing the tone in Erin's voice, lay back down with a harrumph.

"Molly, I just couldn't take a chance to let someone else file on it. I rode all over that place, and I think it just might be perfect. I was on pins and needles as the clerk went through the section and checked the filings. I don't think I've ever wanted anything so badly before in my life."

"Anything?" Molly asked in a voice that had Erin turning towards her quickly.

Taking Molly in her arms, Erin answered huskily, "Well, not just anything." She began to turn her excitement over the land into excitement over making love to her wife, kissing her ardently.

Molly immediately returned her adoration, kissing her back, hard.

Erin realized it had been too long since they'd been alone, neither had their periods, and Molly hadn't been ill. She responded immediately, pulling at Molly's clothes to feel her naked skin against her wife's, pressing close, hearing the catch in her voice at the contact.

Molly had worried at the length of time Erin was gone in search of their homestead and being relieved at her return, as well as overjoyed at her find, she expressed herself physically, wrapping her naked body around her wife, rubbing, and murmuring in enjoyment.

Erin kissed her way across her wife's jaw and down her neck, then paid homage to the breasts standing up and peaking in their excitement. First one, and then the other, received devotion as she licked, sucked, and gently used her teeth. The catch in Molly's breath told her how much her wife was enjoying the attention. Her hands weren't idle as she caressed her wife's luscious curves, remembering how she had looked and felt when they had been able to make love without children nearby.

Molly was enjoying her wife's dedication to giving her enjoyment. She was equally determined to love Erin in return and kissed, suckled, and caressed all the bare skin she could reach.

Erin could scent Molly's arousal and that made her want to taste. She slowly made her way between her wife's legs, pleasantly surprised to find that she had bathed recently, and she was fresh and clean and tasted heavenly. Her first lick had Molly arching into her mouth in supplication.

"More," she gasped, reaching for Erin's head to hold her in place.

Erin smiled against Molly's clit, enjoying herself as she licked away the juices from the appendage that stood at attention waiting for her. Suckling slightly, her fingers slipped inside and made a come-hither motion, bringing Molly up off their blankets only to fall back helplessly as she touched the tender tissue within.

"Oh," she moaned and then stifled it by putting her fist into her own mouth, knowing the children were simply yards away. Her body wasn't under her control as Erin played with it.

Erin began an in and out motion with her fingers, and on every third thrust she 'accidentally' curled them to hit the spot that Molly so enjoyed, causing her to gasp at the sensations that were building. Her mouth gently suckled on Molly's clit as her tongue swirled around it. She could tell from Molly's breathing that her crisis was nearing. She held on as her wife's body convulsed in her arms, smiling as she came not once but twice in succession.

Molly couldn't believe how incredibly her wife aroused her. She hadn't known these feelings were inside herself until Erin taught her so long ago. She'd never thought of touching herself, knowing she was meant to save herself for her someday husband's pleasure. She didn't know the woman could receive pleasure too. Learning that another woman could and would give her pleasure had been a revelation and she reveled in learning her body and its responses. Realizing that Erin was learning as well had been such a delight. They learned together, exploring each other to discover whatever means they could to obtain this pleasure. Finding that she could orgasm, that it wasn't an experience solely for men, had been a revelation. She forced herself to come down from her high quickly, entirely satisfied by what Erin had done to her body as she rolled their heated and sweaty bodies over and began to lave attention on Erin, doing many of the same things to her tall, lanky body in return.

Erin loved this moment when Molly turned the tides of their lovemaking. She was hoping that someday they could come at the same time; she was certain it was possible. She didn't analyze it too strongly as she was enjoying herself far too much to think coherently. Molly had been a willing student, and when she realized Erin was learning too, she became less defensive. As each found what pleased the other, they discovered a part of their love they hadn't known was missing. Now, they had it down pat and could instantly push the other's buttons to quickly arouse them and make them replete. Erin was already aroused from making love to her wife, and it didn't take long for her to come against her wife as she thrust her fingers inside. Seeing her licking them afterwards aroused Erin again, and she took advantage that, rubbing against Molly's leg as she ground herself into completion once more. Molly's answering smile told her it had been deliberate. She turned off the barely lit lantern, so they could go to sleep.

"Maybe I should build a bathhouse first," Erin murmured sleepily afterwards.

"First? Why?"

"So, we can take a hot bath together without the children barging in and seeing us," she answered, tweaking Molly's still hard nipple through the nightclothes she had put back on. She clearly recalled the view of Molly in their house in Ohio, the thin towel barely covering her lush body, her long, dark hair loose about her shoulders. She had modestly tried to cover herself, but the view was forever burned in Erin's mind.

"That sounds wonderful," Molly said as she stretched, not quite as sated from their lovemaking as she had thought. The tweak had caused a corresponding twinge in her crotch, and she really wanted to continue, but they both heard the growls of the dogs.

Erin quickly got dressed and went out, carrying her pistol in her waistband and slinging her rifle over her shoulder as she peered through the darkness to see what the dogs were upset about. It was difficult to see as the moon was behind some clouds, but she could hear the dogs on the far side of the herd. She could see the silhouettes of the cattle all looking off to the west. Billy snorted a challenge of sorts, letting whoever or whatever know he was ready for them and willing to fight. Walking slowly, so she wouldn't spook the animals, she found both dogs alert and posing, looking off into the night. They had stopped growling. Erin quietly petted both dogs, praising them for she knew not what. Still, whatever had upset them might be gone. When she could see the cattle cropping grass again and the hackles on the dogs had gone down, she started to make her way back to their camp.

"What was it?" Molly asked, having pulled on more clothing just in case she was needed. Her shotgun was nearby and ready.

"I don't know, but whatever it was wasn't willing to take on the dogs and Billy."

Molly didn't blame whoever or whatever it was. She wouldn't like her odds either if those three came at her. "Do you think someone was trying to see if they could get our cattle?"

"I don't know," she admitted. She was tired now, and all thoughts of further lovemaking were gone from her mind as she worried about

taking her family to the remote area of Oregon she had filed on. They would have to get supplies soon but only after she had built them a strong cabin against the winter snows. She had heard it didn't snow in certain parts of Oregon but having seen some of the mountains they came through, she was pretty sure it would snow where they were. She would soon need the money she had forwarded to Oregon and wondered how long it would take to arrive after the letter she had sent. She heard Molly snoring slightly and decided she would join her after she mentally thought through the building of their cabin. It took a while to walk herself through that. She had never built a cabin but had listened avidly as the settlers and mountain men in their wagon train had spoken of it in detail. She knew the cabin couldn't be very big. She wasn't certain she could do it, but she had to try; she had promised them all a home.

~ ~ ~ ~ ~

They packed up the next morning. It was odd how alone and different camping felt since the wagon train had moved on. Putting the cages of poultry up on the sides of the wagon, she was disappointed to find one of the chickens dead. Still, they had suffered relatively few losses, and not counting those marked for eating, they had a lot of stock left to rebuild their flocks. They put the chicken in a bag to be plucked and baked later for their dinner.

Erin walked a wide arc with the dogs, who snuffled avidly, but she saw no signs of man or beast that might have caused the animals to become upset the previous night. Returning to the fire, she shrugged at Molly's look.

The children asked a million and one questions until Erin shushed them. She was concentrating on keeping the cattle at a walk on the odd trail she had taken in the previous days. There wasn't an obvious wagon trail south from where they were heading, and she worried if they would be able to get through in a couple places or if they could become lost. Still, their teams and both sets of yoked oxen were strong and pulling the Conestoga wagon effortlessly across the land didn't seem to faze them. She watched as the pigs kept up easily under the back of the wagon in their accustomed place.

There was plenty to graze when they stopped that first night, and the animals fell to cropping it as quickly as they could. The children were disappointed that they weren't on 'their' land that first night, but Erin explained that a horse and rider could travel much faster alone than their large wagon and all these animals.

On the second day, Erin had to ride ahead a bit to make sure they were on the right path. She hoped her memory of the previous trip was accurate. Some of the trail wasn't good for the wagon, and they had to be creative in how they got through, around, and over some of the obstacles.

"Come on, you can do it," she encouraged the teams as they pulled up a rather steep grade. She saw Theo, who was walking, had stopped the flock of sheep behind them, waiting to follow the large wagon. She looked farther behind him and Tabitha was sitting on the mare and

signaling to King to slow the cattle, who took advantage of the moment to crop at the grass.

It started raining as they drove along that afternoon, and they had to make camp in the rain that night. It wasn't a gentle rain. They had been warned that some of the rains were coming in off the ocean and would hit the mountains west of them, including Mount Hood, which was now north and west of them. Erin thought about that far-off mountain they said had been a volcano once. She wondered what would happen if it went off. She'd heard stories of volcanoes but had never seen one. It sounded like they must be like the fires of hell.

Coping in the rain, nothing new after their long trip out here, they made a small fire and used lard to cook the chicken, so they could all have a hot meal. Erin had rigged the awning off the wagon, so they could have the fire and keep a relatively rain-free space. The smoke went out both sides of the awning as it flapped in the wind. As she ate, she watched the ducks and geese stretching their necks out beyond the cages trying to catch some water and pecking at the grasses they were placed in to find things only they could see. She was looking forward to getting them out of the cages but wondered at how vulnerable they would be out on the farm, especially in an area that had never seen domesticated animals and birds before.

"It isn't going to be a farm with that many acres," Molly teased her as they wearily got ready for bed. The children had been tucked into both the wagon and the other tent that night. The cats weren't liking having to share 'their' beds in the wagon again.

"Oh, what is it then?" Erin asked, pulling at her boot and pleased when Molly brushed aside her hand to pull on it for her. Her shapely derriere was a fine sight in the low light of the lantern. Erin helped push on the boot with her other booted foot and pointed the toe on the foot between Molly's legs. The boot came off easily with their combined efforts, and Molly took one unbalanced step before turning for the other boot. Both boots were soon off.

"With that many acres, it's a ranch," she contended.

"I think it's a farm or a ranch, whatever we *want* to call it." She pulled off her pants and changed her shirt for a men's nightshirt, doing it quickly, so her bindings wouldn't be exposed too long. That was something she had done many times on the trail until it became automatic.

They chuckled at their teasing, eager to get to their new home, but a wagon was slow traveling, and it took days.

TO BE CONTINUED...

~End sample chapter of PIONEERING~
For more go to www.Shadoepublishing.com to purchase
the complete book or for many other delightful offerings

~ Because a publisher should stand behind their authors~

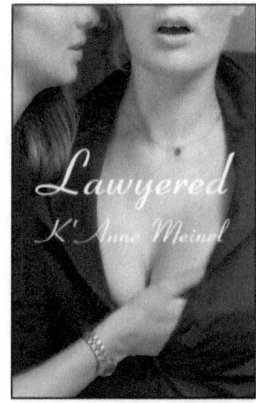

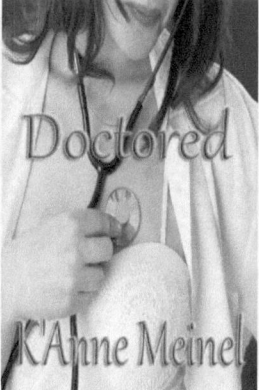

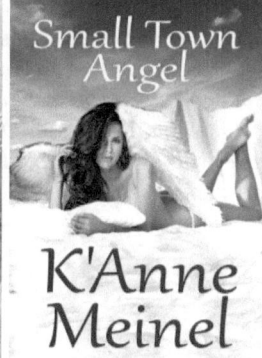

www.shadoepublishing.com

~ Because a publisher should stand behind their authors~

What do you do when you meet someone who changes everything you know about love and passion?

Paige Harlow is a good girl. She's always known where she was going in life: top grades, an ivy league school, a medical degree, regular church attendance, and a happy marriage to a man. Falling in love with her gorgeous roommate and best friend Alyssa Torres is no small crisis. Alyssa is chasing demons of her own, a medical condition that makes her an outcast and a family dysfunctional to the point of disintegration make her a questionable choice for any stable relationship. But Paige's heart is no longer her own. She must now battle the prejudices of her family, friends, and church and come to peace with her new sexuality before she can hope to win the affections of the woman of her dreams. But will love be enough?

~ Because a publisher should stand behind their authors~

In the male dominated sport of Formula 1 racing, Samantha 'Sam' Dupree is struggling to make her mark against the boys. She hears about a driver who is making a name for herself in NASCAR and goes to check her out. Little does she know that she's in for the race of her heart.

Addison McCloud wants nothing more than to drive. She doesn't care about fame or fortune; she just wants to be fast enough to get herself and her family away from her abusive father. Meeting Sam, changes her world and revs her life into overdrive.

When the two women meet, sparks flies like the race cars that they drive. Will they be able to steer their relationship into something more and win the race, or will their families make them crash and burn. The boys of Formula 1 are going to learn that Southern girls are a force to be reckoned with.

~ Because a publisher should stand behind their authors~

Carrie flees from the demons of her present, trying to protect the ones she loves.

Frankie hides from the demons of her past, and the memory of loved ones she failed to protect.

A modern day princess thrown to the wolves, Carrie's only hope is the rancher who had spent the better part of a decade in self imposed, near total, isolation. Frankie's history of losing those she tries to save haunts her, but this madman threatens her home, her livestock, her sanctuary. She knows she can't do it alone, has she still got enough support from her oldest friends?

Amelia Gittens had the credit of being the first and only woman thus far in the United States military of being a sniper in combat, made possible by being in the Military Police unit of the crack 10th Mountain Infantry Division. After retirement she joins the City of New York Police Department, and suddenly finds herself involved in a suspect shooting incident which soon encroaches upon her entire life. In order to protect her therapist who has been targeted as a revenge killing, Amelia takes on the responsibility as if she was still in the Army, treating it as a tactical maneuver.

~ Because a publisher should stand behind their authors~

When U.S. Marine Dakota McKnight returned home from her third tour in *Operation Iraqi Freedom*, she carried more baggage than the gear and dress blues she had deployed with. A vicious rocket-propelled grenade attack on her base left her best friend dead and Dakota physically and emotionally wounded. The marine who once carried herself with purpose and confidence, has returned broken and haunted by the horrors of war. When she returns to the civilian world, life is not easy, but with the help of her therapist, Janie, she is barely managing to hold her life together...then she meets Beth.

Beth Kendrick is an American history college professor. She is as straight-laced as they come, until Dakota enters her life, that is. Will her children understand what she is going through? Will she take a chance on the broken marine or decide to wait for the perfect someone to come along?

Time is on your side, they say, unless there is a dark, sinister evil at work. Is their love strong enough to hold these two people together? Will the love of a good woman help Dakota find the path to recovery? Or is she doomed to a life of inner turmoil and destruction that knows no end?

www.shadoepublishing.com

If you have enjoyed this book and the others listed here
Shadoe Publishing, LLC is always looking for first, second, or
third time authors. Please check out our website @
www.shadoepublishing.com
For information or to contact us @
shadoepublishing@gmail.com.

We may be able to help you bring your dreams of becoming a
published author to life.

www.ingramcontent.com/pod-product-compliance
Lightning Source LLC
Chambersburg PA
CBHW050937120626
46552CB00001B/254